Drunken Baker

Barney Farmer

Drunken Baker
Barney Farmer

ISBN 978-1-903110-54-6

First published in this edition 2018 by Wrecking Ball Press.

Illustrations by Barney Farmer and Dave Iddon

Book design by humandesign.co.uk

Printed and bound in Great Britain by Clays Ltd, St Ives plc

Supported using public funding by
ARTS COUNCIL ENGLAND
LOTTERY FUNDED

For fuck's sake.

Must be getting time to think about making a move.

In a minute or two. Finish this first, then have a look.

Christ I'm tired. Should have got some sleep. Or more sleep.
Must have got a bit of sleep, because I don't remember
getting on the floor, but nowhere near enough.

Should have turned out the light and closed the curtains. Gone up.
When the wine went was when I should have gone up.

Tired enough then. Could have slept 20 hours and never dreamed.
No need of a night-cap. Well away. Out on my feet. Shuddering.

That thing when it feels like there's water racing though your legs.
Do you get that? I never used to.

But you open the next one and you're into it.
And this is a nice drop, to be fair. A good rum, this is.

Warming not hot, rich and sweet, not sickly.

I'll take the rest into work. No I won't. So I can put it down,
turn my back, and that cunt can neck it?
He can fuck off.

Creep out, close the door, softly softly sneck clicks in latch.
Habit really. I was married wasn't I? Long time ago now.

Eight-odd year or so tiptoeing, a little 'un sleeping
in the front box room right over the door for most of that,
and since then I never think about it, I just leave quiet.

Nice cold air on that breeze, blow some wool out me head.
Mmm, I can feel my face...
Months going faster every day aren't they?
Already stopping darker later, getting darker sooner, later on.

No odds to me. Used to starting in the dark, me, any road,
bar them mornings in summer, just now gone, when you
clock orange and purple fingers reaching up over the rooftops.

Still the middle of the night for you,
but my morning since I was young,
younger than you are now.
Your mornings are my afternoons.
Your afternoon is my night.
Your evening is my night, still.

And this is the way I've always walked.
This way, through these streets, all them years, all on my own,
all alone in the dark and the quiet.

Only my footsteps or the odd piss-head rolling home break the silence.
Or a clink in the bag. If I take a bag. Sometimes there's stuff in.

Everyone asleep bar me, is how it feels. Bar us, I mean.
Bar us bakers.

Be same story all over the world. Even the postmen are still in their
beds, not earning their daily bread.
We'll be making that fucking bread mate, from here to Timbuktu.
And the cakes, such as we do these days.
No pies. No savouries. Had to stop. Must be months now, since.
All getting wasted, every crumb.
We can't compete with them shitty chains. We can't make a go.
We've them ten-bob pasty bastards one end of town to the other.

Used to be just the one, the famous one, and just that for ages,
in the precinct, but last ten year or so the fuckers pop up like
mushrooms, cheaper and cheaper, shitter and shitter an' all, but
cheaper.

Two steak slice for a quid? A fucking quid? That's us fucked there.

And steak? Get to fuck is steak, I don't know how they get away with
it. Where's fucking Trading Standards?

It's bleeding shit, bought by the tonne, blasted off of fucking skeletons
with a jet-wash, but people see that word 'steak' and think 'oooooo I
deserve a treat, I've earned a treat sat on me arse'.

Maybe you do, maybe you don't, but you ain't fucking getting one.
They seen you coming. You've been fucking had pal.

So we stopped. We had to stop. There's only so much you can throw
in the bin. Or eat yourself. And I can't eat any of it much,
can't keep it down the same.

What is it if you see a run over black cat? Lucky or unlucky?
Can't cross my path so lucky I suppose. Or is it lucky if they do?
Somebody'll be unhappy whatever. Nice someone pulled it out of road,

stop it getting chewed up more for the owner.

Miles more cats I see now, on the way. Spying from under cars,
peering down from wall ends, snotty bastards.

Less birds. That's them. Bastards. Trees bustling with birds some
mornings once. Some still are to be fair. Some cats are alright.

The missus got a cat. Never took to me. They took it with 'em.
You know how sometimes cats what get moved travel miles
get back to their old home?
This never.

Couldn't tell you how many foxes I seen.
Thousands. Fucking heads jammed in a bin-bag half the time.

None today, not yet, but get the fried chicken stretch there'll be one, I
bet, and a shitload of rats.

Always been a few of them, always, the canal's just there,
always has been, but they're thriving now.

Used to see a few deer.

Glimpses, here and there. Flitting across the corner of your eye.
Disappearing. They hear you from miles off.

A stag, once, just the once, and that was bang middle of that road,
down there, bold as brass, staring right at us, right into my eyes as
I come round the corner, like the fucker had been waiting for me
forever.

Big bastard an' all, horns and the lot. Took one step toward us and
I slung the bottle, hard as I could, and it smashed on a car, sprayed
sherry at his feet.

Had a sniff of it, gawped a minute, then strolled off, no worries, between the houses, towards the gasometer.

Course, the town's grown since then.
Half again, doubled, more,
shot out every side.
All them orange houses,
the pokey little shitholes
where big fields used to start.

Fucking thousands. Sling up another hundred every time you turn around. None of the people in 'em work here.
There's nothing to do is there?

But they built a new junction, and that made this town into somewhere you can live on the edge of and get out.

Most never get nearer town centre than the retail park they built by the bypass, with the fuck-off massive ADLD and them outlets.

Can't blame 'em, there's fuck all left. Bled us all, that park.
All the little shops, one by one.

The Precinct is empty past Boozeland, bar SUPACIGS and charity
shops, and them like jumble sales, full of stretched shit, an' all.

I got a like new Abercrombie overcoat there once for a fiver way
back when, but last I looked it was twatted paperbacks and rags.

Stained things.

Any road, whatever, if deer do still wander in from off the tops,
out of the woods, they don't come this far no more.
Be away walking the rows and rows of houses where fields they
used to fuck in are, if at all, over there, or over that way.

Stag stares across ADLD car park,
waiting for somebody else, not me.
Their frozen fuckin' dough thawer
and pie warmer-upper, maybe.
Up and over the canal bridge, where that poor woman
run off with our gin that time after he...
And drowned, we found out, we never knew for ages,
we'd only met her that day, he had, not me.
I wanted nothing to do with the daft cow.

And down the hill, light of the bakery shining up from way off down
there,
all the way down the bottom of the hill, corner of Bird Street,
straight as a die, right down the end, a tiny beacon, as was.

Something to make for when you was perishing in winter. But not
much now. Cunt never keeps hold of a key more than two minute, so
either I get in first or it's downhill to a dark shape.

Dark now, light back then,

always light, with the gaffer,
but hardly ever after.
Gleamed through the gloom every day,
and noisy from hundred yard away.

Bashing tins, the gaffer banging on, swearing, but never the really bad
stuff, never, bloody, bugger, arsehole, sod off, that stuff, no fucking
or nothing,
half the time arguing with Alice and her arguing back even louder,
both of 'em laughing.

Then him booming 'Where the bloody hell have YOU been?'
when you duck in, early, bang on time, late, only once or twice,
when the little 'un was poorly or I'd had a skinful, something like.

His way of saying hello and get your arse in motion, always the same.
And I mean always. Never took one day's holiday off that man,
that I know of, unless he might have been off when I was off,
and I don't reckon he was.

Sundays and Christmas and Easter and all them, that's all he took.

Never been in the bakery without him in it until the first day in after
his last day in the shop, and the day before that was first day I ever
seen him ill!
Never got ill. But he was bloody ill. Pale and moaning about his eye,
talking like he was pissed, puking, sweat pissing out of him,
hair like he'd climbed out of the bath...
So aye, arse in motion before you got your coat off.
Jumper off in winter, shirt off in summer, trousers too, some
summers, that bad drought, you had to, you couldn't be in there
towards noon with that heat, them old coke ovens, with nothing on,
and straight to work.
Never should have ripped them out, I told him.
Dry heat.

Four of us in the back then, me, the gaffer, that cunt, but I was here
before him, a fucking year before him, there was an old fella who
retired, and the other lad started just after me.

What was his name...

Big sod. Didn't stop long. Four or five year? Joined up, him,
1970-something, eight or nine. Went to Ireland and come back
a different sort of lad, then the Falklands, and come back
all over the fucking show.

We seen him once.
What was his name?
Built like a brick shithouse.
Quiet as a church mouse,
before he went away.
Topped his self last year,
or the year before that,
wife had gone I'd heard.
My wife went.
Both of them went.

Four of us, baking for the shop and the orders, pubs and clubs, hotel
or two.

Hard graft, boiling, red-faced, swinging sacks, sifting, kneading,
slicing dough, filling tins, hot, loud, clanging, piss-wrapped sweat
head-to-toe,
swilling tea by the gallon.
Alice kept the brews coming, the gaffer's wife Alice, she ran the front,
the serving, and if not her one of her lasses,
all lasses, well, I say lasses, most of 'em knocking on.
Old hands, worked with Alice a long while one or two. Carole was one,
her son was one of them autistics and fucking run her ragged.
Florence, with her rosy cheeks and wall-eyes, she was a young 'un.

There were others, they come and went.

My mother, for a bit, before me, although she done her bit in the back too as she had very cold hands and was good with the dainty cakes an' all.

She'd have kept the tea flowing out back too though, for some other grafting blokes, her or one of the other lasses, while they was getting set for opening.

Kettle hardly stopped singing in there, then, when the flour was flying and drying you out and the big coke ovens was coming up.

Fine flour floats,
on swirling hot air,
white eyes and hair,
nose full of bread proving,
baking or cooling,
every breath was bread.

So you had a thirst. You had a biting –
There he is, the cunt. The fucking cunt.

Not the same rush now. No rush at all really.
Arse in slow motion is plenty. No shouting or banging,
no pissing sweat, nor Alice and the lasses out front.
A kettle ain't sung in this place since we started having a drink,
a proper drink, without hiding it, and earlier than we had before.

Ha ha, Alice ain't been in this shop 20 year! More. Is it? Must be.
Fuck knows. Long before the gaffer went I know that.

I know she went went, pegged it, last year.
No, the year before.

I went the church. He didn't.
Come out with his usual about how she was a hard-faced cow,
who'd slagged him to the gaffer, for fuck all,
so fuck her, and she'd never liked him,
or give him a chance,
nor the gaffer.

He was wrong.

Alice give him a fucking chance like she give everyone a chance.
You only got one chance to throw it back in her face, though,
and then you were done.

Not the same rush, no, not now.
Nobody going be standing at the door come eight with errands to run,
tut-tutting and pointing at their watch through the window.

Not be a line along the pavement, along the street, past the bookies,
down to the hairdressers week up to Christmas, some years,
nattering headscarves and smoking fags.

Same faces same days week after week,
regular orders, the most part.

Be 99 out of hundred of 'em women, only one or two blokes,
older ones too, widowers and them.
Never seen many men under 60 until gone noon, then them in for
the pies.
Every morning be a queue out front, the early birds, the older girls,
who got the habit of shopping early doors, from all them years of
rationing.

Same faces, same times, same orders, this, that, treats, basics,
but always two large white, three large white, four large white.

Every day the large white flew.

We done a bit of brown. That advert with the lad on the bike going up
the hill done a fair bit for that, but even then. We done it but nobody
apart from dieters and nut-munchers wanted it.

Nobody apart from them wants it now, ask me. Fucking idiots force
it down. Good white's as good for you, they can fuck off, it is.

Spun up in tissue,
away down the street,
still hot in your hands,
water, mould, wheat.

Everyone got their bread here.

Everyone bar lazy gets who wouldn't walk past Crooks in King Street.
They was second best bakers in town but their bread was nothing
next to ours, palsied shite, and dearer an' all.

Their pies were alright though. Can't knock them. But pies aren't
bread, and everyone always needs bread, and theirs was shit.
Lazy bastards was welcome to it.
They only opened in the 19-fucking-60s.
Our large white was old by then, already.

Tried and true, it'd been coming hand to hand, father to son,
this is the way we make bread, for fucking years.
Fucking generations.

The gaffer's dad was a baker before him, see, in this shop, and his
dad's dad a baker before that, same shop, all that's changed is the
ovens, electric now, not coke. Should never have fucking got rid...
Bread of that family fed this town for 70 years. More. I had that large
white mashed in milk before there was a fucking tooth in my head,
my mother said.

The gaffer was sterile though and the end of the line. So he showed
me what he'd have showed his own. And he showed that cunt an' all.

This is the way we make our bread.

I can taste it now.
We don't make it now.
Nobody wants it now.

That old mix comes out £1.60 a loaf if we're going to make a go of it,
and fuckers are getting a sliced white in ADLD for half a quid, less,
if they need.

Bendy, gummy, tastes like shit, is shit, but does a job if you're counting
the pennies, and that's a life's work for most people round here, and
for a fucking long time an' all.

Not that I think nobody round here wants good bread, at a fair price,
older ones who remember when good bread was a fair price.
Maybe they do but can't afford it no more, any price.

And the younger 'uns, half of them, to them,
we're just some dirty old shop on a dirty street.

Them who never queued here in the rain holding their mum's hand

bored out of their head, or pressed their little nose against the glass and drooled over the trifles, or had their arses tanned for acting the goat in the shop, or had Alice come round the counter,
give 'em a little piece of cake, just for them.

The little pieces, the little links are broke, for good an' all.

So now we cut a few corners, we have to, to keep going. Cheaper this, cheaper that, you'd never tell unless you're used to right good bread, but it's not that bread, not the old bread, not the bread that fed the town, can't be, not anymore, so nobody goes out their way for it.
Quid a loaf best we can do. And shift next to fuck all anyway truth told. Out on a limb, here, now.

Used to be the big factory down the bottom, dozen or so shops stretched along the street, engineering place three streets over, 100-odd in there, all the warehouses along the canal had people in them.

We're the last stop on a long shit street, pair of ten-bob pasty bastards between us and the town centre, and one of 'em not fifty fucking paces up the fucking row.

"You having a brandy then?"

What was the town centre. Is bloody depressing now.

"Yeah, and a large one an' all, I feel fucking dreadful."

Why'd I say that?

"First let's be on with the bread."

"Yeah, then the cakes."

Pissed-up cunt ain't made a cake you'd want to touch with your foot in 10 years. Look at the shake on him. He's younger than me, just.

Put lard in Victoria sponge shitfaced yesterday then screamed fucking murder when some woman fetched her slice back. Because she'd fetched it back. She won't be fucking back.

"And jam tarts."

Jam tarts? Him? Don't make me laugh.
What can go wrong with a jam tart? What d'you reckon?
Sweet pastry and jam, that's all. Easy.
Well just you watch that cunt make a jam tart.
Tell you this, nothing never used to go wrong with our jam tarts.
They were special, I'm telling you, one of our specialities.
People travelled miles for the bastards, shit you not.
People bought 'em by the dozen, they was stuffing them down
their selves out the bag before they were out the fucking shop.

Get the pastry right and you're laughing. That's the secret.
Jam is just jam, no odds so long as it's not that pure shit.

So is lemon curd.

Butter. Sugar. Flour. Eggs.
Pinch of salt. Simple.
Sift the flour.
Knife the butter through it.
Crumb it.

Never used the claw, always me hands, cold as fuck like mum.
Sugar. Egg. Mix 'til stiff. Splash of water. Knead. Fridge for ten minutes.
Roll, cut, bake it a bit.

Some don't, we did, makes 'em a bit crisper, just five minute,
add jam, bake to a finish.

Swear the gaffer's sweet pastry would be best you ever tasted,
sweet, not too sweet, and broke just right,

and like all the tricks and craft his dad and grandad passed to him,
he passed that on to us.

When and how you add the eggs, that's the fucking key, but that's
the stuff you take to your grave or else who's going to buy a jam tart
off you?

Simple as tying your slip-on shoes.
But like anything simple is simple to fuck up.

For this cunt it is anyhow.

His hands are too hot,
so fucked before he's opened an egg.
Fucked from square one.
Fucked before he crawls out of bed.
Butter melting second he shoves his hands in the bowl to get rubbing.
Fucked on scones too, self-same reason.

Made no odds, got away with it when we had the machine.
But that's gone fucked long since, so he fell back on the claw.
And then he lost the fucking claw.

Definitely him, 'cos I've never needed it. Always been happy take the
extra few minutes and put my cold hands in.

Any road, now he's fucked every way up, pastry AND scones.

And even though my hands are so cold you'd think I was dead
we're fucked, because I ain't making all that pastry AND scones
all the time.
And he can't, not now we've no machine or even a claw.
But I'll make some jam tarts today. I like a jam tart.
I can keep a jam tart down.

"I'll do the cakes and some jam tarts, you see to the bread."

"You see to the fuckin' bread! What do you reckon of this brandy? I don't think it's the worst. For the price."

Fucking hell I'd forgot it was brandy, is so fucking raw. First gobful hit back of my throat and bounced. Had to clench me fucking head not to spray that and more in his face.

"It'll do, I ain't complaining."

"Good I got a case. Dozen bottles fifty quid off that fat bastard with the van. He reckons they was meant for export but the warehouse burned down."

"Where's he parking now?"

"Behind the old bus garage, right up against the wall. You can't see him unless you walk right down the side."

Big pull on the bottle, up to the vertical, eyes pissing,
apple thumping up and down, and that gurgling he does.

"Don't put the bottle in your horrible gob."

"I forgot."

Sipping shit like this is the way. Just sip, sip, and it really ain't so bad at all.

I've had worse. First impressions can be wrong with cheaper spirits, have a bit more, quick, and they improve.
And less than five quid a bottle, what do you want?

I wouldn't go near it at home like. But work.

"We should make a batch of them little buns we used to do with the buttercream in 'em, and the lid chopped in half and stuck in the buttercream on 'em."

Butterfly buns. He means butterfly buns.

Used to sell plenty, a little treat for the old dears whose pension didn't run to an éclair or a bit of Battenberg.

Most old people were skint, then, people forget that now.
Well, they wasn't skint, they just wasn't rolling about
in open-topped sports cars with suntans.

It's their kids, what are old now, that have all the money, and they don't come this end of town.
Don't live round here in any numbers really.
But a pain in the arse and can't make a cake don't keep more than two days on the shelf. Buttercream goes funny. Since the cold cabinet went fucked.

That's why we don't do cream no more neither. Two hour it's cheese.

"Butterfly buns."

"Buttercream, y'deaf cunt."

"The butterfly bit is the cut-out bits in the buttercream that look like wings."

"Fuck me they do an' all! I always wondered what the fuck people was on about..."

'Butterfiles' my little girl used to call them,
when she were little.
Last time I seen her.
'Butterfile cake, Daddy!
She hadn't much started school.

Quietly top up and leave the babbling cunt at it. Soon as this glass is gone I'm after a can or something.

Gone six and all we've done is drink brandy and talk shit. Which isn't bad, once you get the taste.

And five quid...

I'll do four cakes. Four different cakes.
Not a bad offer for a Wednesday, that, with the bits left from yesterday.
The macaroons will be okay. The ginger cake.
They was tinned up nice and tight. Few odds and sods. Viennese Fingers?

And half will go in the bin any road. More.

A Dundee cake.
A dozen slice, quid a slice, good big slice, nobody's complained yet.
It's a solid cake, tin that up when we shut tonight,
good for four days as fresh.
The old 'uns like Dundee cake an' all,
and they're about the only fuckers come in here.
The skint ones.

The housewives all go ADLD, pie-eaters go the ten-bob twats,
we're left with the old and them as can't get.

Too far to walk.
Buses are dear.
Don't worry love,
we're still here,
we're going nowhere.

Some of 'em probably coming in for years, but I was mostly in the back
until all the lasses went, and their faces don't mean a thing to me.

No kids ever. Ever. Last time we had a kid in, and this was fucking
years ago, this, little bastard threw a banger at that cunt and it got
stuck in his hair.

Blew him a big bald patch just over his ear,
knocked him deaf for a week. I was fucking howling.

Used to be full of kids, squawking and arsing about,
good few from the high school having a pie at dinnertime.

But none now. Never.

My little 'un loved coming in here.
No wonder, all the lasses out front fussing round her while she begged
for bits of cake like she didn't get enough at home.
Kids don't go mad for cakes these days, not like we did,
not from a craftsman baker.

Times change. When I was a kid, starting here, washing tins Saturday
morning for a few nicker, all I was thinking about was what cakes'd
be going spare when Alice turned the sign over, 1pm sharp.

Everyone working got a bit of anything left, and there was never much,
but she had a soft spot for me and I'd always get first pick. I had this

long brown straight hair back then and she said I was a little Beatle.

Course I should have gone seen her more, once the gaffer had gone,
but work just gets on top of you, you know, when there's only two
of you,
and I never gone at all after the funeral.

Victoria sponge. Two if we've the stuff. Piece of piss, any leftover
chopped up in the trifle bases once it's gone, and if you don't put
cream in that's a few day off.

Scones. Cheap and cheerful, good as fresh for two day, and mine are
good. Fucking good. A natural, the gaffer, told me, first bite.

If I took 'em on that British baking thing they'd fuckin' send everyone
home, all of 'em, fuck off out of it!
Cold hands. I'm lucky with that. Melt the butter before your crumb's
there and your scones will be heavy, bit waxy against your teeth.

Not me, my crumbs are lovely to see, run your hand through 'em,
feel 'em slip through your fingers, golden and soft.
Dozen cherry, dozen sultana. We'll sell a few. I'll eat a few.
They'll go over two day.

And a dozen individual trifles. They ain't cakes, really, but they're
something. We've that lardy sponge to use up.
Get that broke in some jelly, sharp, get set.

This brandy is okay. At the price. I'll take one home.
He fucking will be.

"How many large white'm I making?"

"A dozen? 20? How many we sell yesterday?"

"Fuck all."

"Do a dozen."

The shit they put out for Dundee cake these days is a disgrace. Any old bit of fruitcake flogged as Dundee cake, these days. They want fucking necking.
I don't blame the cunts selling,
everyone has to live,
I blame the cunts buying,
who knew the difference once,
and have fuck all to gain from forgetting.

For one, Dundee cake ain't got fucking cherries in it. Or raisins, for another. Queen Mary didn't like fucking cherries, that's the thing.

I seen that written on a tea-towel.

Sultanas and orange rind is your fruit, that's all, not just what you bloody want. You wouldn't put coffee in a chocolate éclair.
Well you could but it'd be a coffee fucking renoir.

Dundee cake should be a bit bittersweet not a gobful of sugar.
Shot of whisky in it an' all, the gaffer done, lift it right up,
and so did we, but we've no whisky about.

We'll never have no whisky about.

"Have we any whisky about?"

"Have we?"

"For the Dundee cake."

"I'll have a glass."

Brandy'll have to do for that. It'll do. Got to have almonds on top.
They're there for cherries in the old story.

See one without almonds and it's a fruitcake.
They're both fruitcake. But only one's a fucking Dundee cake.

"Is it a single malt? Cos I prefer Bells these days."

"There isn't any fuckin' whisky!"

Crunchy almonds, baked golden brown on top.
Looks lovely that. Always my favourite an' all.
Slice of Dundee cake in my little butty box all the way through school,
buttered if it was knocking on a bit, or it sucked your gob dry.

Always seemed to be one in the tin. As I say, a decent keeper.

Mum made a good Dundee cake.
Should have been, it was the gaffer's Dundee cake. She done a stint
here when she first left school, until I come along, baking and serving.

Her gaffer wasn't our gaffer, her gaffer was my gaffer's dad, right near
the end, when he was slowing down.
He was long gone by time I come in,
but he still come in, now and then,
tell our gaffer what he was doing wrong, which was everything, he
reckoned.

Same Dundee cake though. It was older than them two an' all.

My gaffer's dad's dad's. Marmalade's the difference.
Two tablespoon darkest coarse cut you can get, ounce of sugar less
for it.

My gaffer did run the back back then though, when mum was here,
back when it was half again busier than I ever knew it,
and there was half again as many bodies, just in the back.

So mum was here, so that's how I got the Saturday job.

Dragged me along one day, stuck her head in, and went out the back with Alice. I heard 'em laughing and talking and when they come out front I was the new tin lad.

'Be here at 5 Saturday morning John Lennon...'

"Is this fucking salt?"

Cunt waving the fucking caster sugar shaker at me,
same shaker we've had forever, white, big black letters on it,
C-A-S-T-E-R.

"Sugar."

"Where's the bottle? We've no salt."

"Look in that cupboard."

"What you put the brandy in there for?"

"Salt. The brandy's in your other fucking hand."

"This brandy's giving me a fucking headache, is it you?"

He's purple the cunt.

"Have a can, I am."

"I'll be having a can."

"What have we?"

"I'll finish off the brandy..."

'Butterfiles'...
I wonder what she calls them now?

Butterflies.
She's 35. No, six.
It's 2016.

"There's no fuckin' salt in there."

"That's salt. There."

"Oh aye. You want Kestrel, or there's one Tennents?"

Fucking supers.

"They cold?"

"They're not hot."

Fucking hate warm supers. Malty glue.

"Give us Tennents."

"Oh fuck off, Kestrel's shit."

"They're both shit, warm."

"Have Kestrel then."

"Who the fuck bought Kestrel anyway?"

"They was 12 for ten."

"Fuckin' drink 'em then."

"I couldn't really give a fuck, pal."

For fuck's sake. Specials are shite warm.
Don't refresh me. Ice cold, it goes easier, if you throw it back.
Warm just coats your trap in malt.
And I hate malt, the taste and the smell. Always have.
We had a brewery corner of our street when I was growing up,
couldn't help but pass it on the way going anywhere.

Every day, before the brewery went, clouds of thick malty steam,
boiling up through holes in the road.
Sometimes got in the house, with a fair wind. Turned my guts.

Good beer they done, I found out, years on, that best bitter.
But good riddance, that bloody stink.

"None been in the fridge?"

"These was in the fridge."

"Don't feel like it."

"Well, the fridge is fucked."

Yes, the fridge is fucked. Opened it yesterday and it was fucked.
We need someone to come out.

"Oh give me the fuckin' Kestrel..."

Fucked like everything else in here, more or less. Only waiting on the
ovens to go now and we can turn out the lights. Nothing new in here
for a long while. Nothing new since they carried the gaffer out feet first.
Just me and him, more or less, since then, nothing new.

"Y'know, if the council come round that's us shut."

"Fuck! When?"

"When what?"

"Sneaky cunts! How long we got?"

"Until what?"

"They fuckin' shut us!"

"They ain't been round."

"You fuckin' on about then?"

What am I fucking on about? Wasting my puff on this cunt.

"Fuck off back to your bread."

Cunt, I've a Dundee cake to get going.

"Stick the fuckin' oven on."

"It is fuckin' on..."

Soft brown sugar, eggs, sultana, self-raising, butter.
Butter.

The fridge is fucked. The butter's gone. Rancid. Must be. Mind it must
have been alright to use yesterday, and the door's been shut since.
That'll've kept the cool in.
Not cold, but don't need to be. Cool is enough.

Nah, it's fucking rancid. Can't put rancid butter in a cake to sell.
Not after that wedding. Them fuckers'd been on the lash too though.
Not all that mess was on us.
It'll be right.

That dough he's laid out proving smells too heavy by half. Don't

smell right.
A bit dank, of cellars.

Should be cleaner. Bit of fresh dug earth.
Should be just a little bit sharp, bit sweet.
I know that smell better than I know fresh air, and that ain't it.

Meant breakfast time once, that smell, get to half-six or so,
when we'd have the whole day's bread laid out to rise.

Pound after pound, all happening inside itself, coming to life, giving
off that perfume. Filled the shop, you could smell it from the yard.

We'd be fags and tea in the yard, cooling down while Alice banged
the bacon on and fried up eggs and tomatoes and slices of yesterday's
bread.

Never fry today's bread, staler the better, you'll find. Same with toast.
But take fresh bread as it comes to you, you can't improve it,
unless it's that gummy supermarket shite.

One last slice to clean the plate, a last fag, then the first lot of dough
what'd got put out should be good to go in, and it'd be all go for an
hour or two.

"Your fuckin' dough stinks rotten."

"I know, fuckin' horrible ain't it?"

"What you put in it?

"Nothing. Yeast didn't smell right neither."

That fridge has been fucked longer than a day...

"It had wet blue dust on it."

And still he put it in. Might as well though.
We haven't any other so fuck all to lose, and it's not as if anyone will
know the difference. It's not as if we'll sell much of it, if any.
Some days none. Not a single loaf of bread.

Into the oven, wet blue dust, cellars and all. Ten minutes on 9, open
door a few minute, bring it down to 5, close the door, another 20
minute.

Maybe it'll bake okay. Give off that perfume what brings people
through the door, even if not to buy bread.

Nobody walks past the smell of bread baking without having their
fucking beak twitch, it's in us over all history.

Don't always get a loaf, but once they're in they have something, take
a slice of Dundee cake home to enjoy over a tea or a warm special or a
mug of whisky.

Good bakeries and chippies are hard to pass, the smells are happy
memories connected straight to your brain.
And time was our bread put hooks in people's noses,
reeled 'em over the threshold.

You'd see fuckers marching along, other way, nothing further from
their minds than a cake, pausing, sniffing, gawping, doubling back,
crossing the road, peering in the window, through the door, up at the
counter, slavering chops, pointing at this and that.
I'll have one of them,
one of those,
what are they?
Two of those...

Ha ha, couldn't help their selves, gannets. Not the same bakery
today though. Not the same people coming by. Six shops on this
street one time.

Just us and the ten-bob bastards right down the end.

Even if they was passing, anyone gets the stink coming out of that oven
in their nose is going to gag. The yeast was bad. Course it was bad.

The fridge is fucked. That dickhead.

Ask myself a thousand times a day why the gaffer brung that cunt
in here.

Well, I know why. I know why because Alice told me why,
I don't remember why, why she told us I mean,
but she'd been bawling and that.

Fucking fostered the cunt hadn't they? For a bit, umpteen year before
he rolled in here looking for a job, when he was 10 or something like.

Sent the little fucker back when he half burned their house down.
Deliberate an' all, but Alice knew she shouldn't have told me that,
and next day told me to say nothing, so I never told nobody.

I told my missus all that, but she never come in here much after that,
so that made no fucking odds. She warned me to steer clear.
Think the gaffer thought he fucking owed him something, even after
what he'd tried to give him, and that cunt knew it well enough.

'Oh he'll be alright, he's a loudmouth that's all,
but if he gets a chance he'll come good.'

Never did. Never will. He's cunt to the marrow.

My business partner. We bought in when the gaffer's health give out.
Decent little concern then, still, easy decision, had to, for our future.
I had a young family to do for.

Borrowed the money, suited and booted down the bank.

Turned out that fucker had borrowed half his half off the fucking gaffer! Got all paid off and clear about the time it started to go fucking tits up.
I'm having a Tennents.

"How long has that had on 9?"

"Has what had?"

"The bread."

"When did it go in?"

"You fuckin' put it in."

"Oh that, yeah..."

"Have you turned it down?"

"Only just gone in."

"When?"

"Er..."

"Get out the fuckin' way."

Already had too long on the hot that. Dark brown tops, by time they done be pitch black. And trust me that smell ain't about to reel nobody in, more drive every fucker away.

Knock it down to 4, give it a slower bake, shove my Dundee at the bottom.
Might as well, is a long 'un. Hour and half, there or thereabouts.

Once that fruit and marmalade warm up it'll take the edge off the

bread stench, the rancid butter an' all, under the sweet and bitter.
And the brandy.
Whisky's better.
But brandy's the same.
Now. Scones.

"Wha' you doing now?"

"Scones."

"I'll give you hand once I've finished this."

Down goes the Tennents. Chug chug chug.
Tennents?
There was only one Tennents half hour ago.
Why am I nursing a fucking Kestrel?

Tennents crushed all over his end. Three, and the one in his hand.

"I thought you said there was only one Tennents."

"No I never."

"You said Kestrel or one Tennents and when I said Tennents you
kicked off and said there was 12 Kestrel."

"There's not now, you've had four."

"How many Tennents is there?"

"Not many."

"How many?"

"Eight."

"You're a cunt mate."

"Ha ha ha ha ha..."

Fucking Tennents cunt!
Cherries and sultanas. Caster. Margarine. Milk. Self-raising. Egg for
the lid. For the shine. Cheapskates use milk, we use egg. Gives a deep
golden top, proper crust, a bite. And the milk'll be fucking off anyhow.
And the marge.
That fucking fridge.

"Ha ha ha ha haaa..."

"Where's them fucking Tennents then?"

"Fridge. I'll get rubbing in some butter for them scones eh?"

"Get the fuck out of them scones."

"I thought you was making jam tarts?"

"I am if you'll fuckin' get –"

Christ that bread stinks. Got to get outside or I'm going to empty
my guts.

"Where you off to?"

"Fuck off."

Sun's up.
Can't see it,
but the clouds are bright.
Pale light over the slates.
Wet slates.
Been raining.

Scrape of a lighter and some cunt coughing his ringpiece out,
just other side of the wall.

Used to enjoy a smoke.
Sitting in the sun.
Tea steaming,
and a few fags,
after breakfast.
Hardest graft just done,
hottest yet to do,
rest of the world half asleep,
trying to catch up with you.

Us young lads opened the gate and watched the lasses head down the
factory for the early shift, whistling and giving 'em fags,
chatting 'em up, all that.

My missus, one of them, for a while, from before she was my missus,
but I never knew her then, and then for a good while when she was,
but not long, she got something better.
Puffing away like us, she was heavy, 30 a day on a good day, we all
must have been fucked.
Until her time was very near, then they was gone.

That's when I give up an' all.

Never heavy like her any road. Ten or so Number 6 a day, or so,
near enough. Them only because I liked the packet.
Dark bottle green and midnight blue striped on white, big gold 6.
Short thin fags, strong tobacco.
Put my last one out 30-odd year ago, never missed 'em.
Needed the money, needed things for that front box room.

The gaffer helped us.
Bits him and Alice had bought but never needed.
Old-fashioned, but so what, they done us.

A coach-built pram weighed like a fucking car.
Shoving that big bastard up the hill and over the canal bridge
near killed me some hot days, with a few inside me!
And they give us a beautiful crib.

Look at all this shit piled out here now.
No lad keeping on top of it for 20 years, see.
First to go when we started letting people go.
That's how they went, one by one.
Until there was just me and that –

"What you doing out here?"

Having a break from you,
in 20 year of rubbish and flour sacks and bust machines,
to get the fuck away from you, for a few minute.

"I'm having five minute."

"I've rubbed some butter up for the scones."

"I said to leave 'em."

"Someone has to fuckin'... Keep stuff moving."

Threads is what'll be in that bowl. Threads of sweaty flour, good for
fuck all.

"It's alright out here ain't it? I never come any more..."

Fuck off don't sit down. Oh for fuck's sake.

"I ain't been out here since we got locked out that time."

"Your bread won't be much longer."

"You broke your arm."

"That was fuckin' you, fallin' off that wall."

"Let's open the gate and watch the scrubbers go down."

"Scrubbers ain't gone down there since the factory shut."

"When'd the factory shut?"

The same time we went from selling a thousand pies a month
to selling fuck all pies a month for fuck's sake.

"Ten year? Twenty? Fuck knows. Long gone."

"I know that, y'prick, just can't remember just when."

"A fuckin' million year for the difference it makes."

Half the blokes in that factory would be up here for our pies,
every day of the week, and that with a subsidised canteen an' all.

Hot plate dinner 20p, my missus reckoned, and still pegged it up
here to give us 22p for a scalding hot mince and onion, or a meat and
potato, or a cheese and onion.
But the fucking mince and onion!
We couldn't keep up, they flew out the door.

Don't do 'em no more so I can tell you the secret.
Fried the onions in dripping, and so long you'd think you've
overdone it,
turning and turning 'em over, then big handful of dark brown sugar,
and turn and turn until they was like oozing treacle,
that was our secret, the Gaffer's secret.

Lift 'em out, don't tip 'em, then brown your mince,

bit by bit, in a bit more dripping and that onion treacle.

Takes a bit longer, but not much, and when you bring it all together that mince and gravy tastes better than any steak you ever had. Is why we only made a few steak and diddley. Nobody wanted 'em, wouldn't pay the extra bob when our mince was that good.

Fucking shop'd be thronging for an hour from noon, mostly blokes, and a swearing line down the road every tick of it.

Alice and the lasses out front like blue-arsed flies they was, Alice cossing all the foul-mouthed bastards and telling 'em to mind their lingo in front of the lasses, then turning the air blue herself if one of 'em dared give her backchat.

They only ever done it the once.
She knew all their mums and wives and birds.
Humping great machine men staring at their boots going 'sorry Alice'.

Made of something special,
she was.
Five foot fuck all,
the gaffer's wife,
seven stone of do not fuckin' mess.

She went before the factory went. Her hands was hurting too much, her fingers got too stiff to be any good for much by then.
All twisted up they were, last I seen her, when the gaffer went.
I held 'em at the chapel and they were lumps of knotted bone.

Big bunch of flowers, huge, they fetched for her, the lasses and the blokes from the factory, mostly the older ones, on her last day.
She'd fed one or two of 'em all their working lives.
She didn't want to go but she was no use.
Never the same in here after that day.

But slow, so you didn't see,
until it was all fucked beyond bringing back.

"Are you going to finish them scones or should I?"

"You've already knackered 'em so you do it. I'll get on them Victoria."

Jesus the cough on that fucker over the wall...

Black ribbons curling from the oven. Now his rotten bread is burning.

"Your bread's burning."

"Get it out for fuck's sake!"

My fucking pleasure you cack-handed bastard.

"Ohhhh, they ain't too bad."

"There's fuckin' smoke coming off 'em!"

"They call that well-fired in the supermarkets, I've seen."

"We call it fuckin' cremated in here."

And now it wants fucking burying.

There's a dozen dead loaves.

There's a dozen loaves nobody is going to put on the table for their family.

Cut a nice thick slice and slap it up with butter and jam and give it their little lass and tell her it's fresh from the jam butty mines and don't tell mum or you'll get no afters.

Made me promise to take her there one day.

She wanted to be a Diddyman. Loved her jam butties.

Only the red jam though. Strawberry. Raspberry. Like everyone.

You don't mind the others but nobody loves the others, not really,

or you'd see apricot or damson in a doughnut, and you never fucking do.

"Some people want it well-fired."

"They ain't well-fired they're fuckin' charcoal."

Well-fired bollocks my arse anyhow,

what they call well-fired in supermarkets

is what once got called 'done', in here,

in any bakery anywhere.

Everything else has been waved at the fucking oven, that's why it's pale as your arse at Christmas and gum in the fucking middle.

Frozen dough off an industrial estate two hundred mile away,

done by the bloody tonne, all machines,

no hands have been in it,

and then maybe not thawed right through before it goes in,

before the oven's just right,

then pulled out too soon 'cos the thing on the oven pinged,

and that means it's ready is all the training they've had.

No crust, half of it, no bite, no flavour. It ain't bread they sell.
I don't know what the fuck it is but it ain't bread.
Mind you neither's these fucking lumps of coal.

"Could be alright once we turn 'em out the tins."

"Aye, some of the ashes might drop off the crust when we flip 'em over."

Flops out the tin, flops in my hand,
flops a dense lump, puff of black dust.
Sharp tap on the arse and it should sound hollow.

Thud. Thud. Thud. Thud. Hollow as a cobble.

The gaffer's bread, the bread we turned out by the thousand loaf
every month, bread we sold by the thousand loaf every month,
bread we could've made fast asleep, once, back then,
tapping the arse of that was like tapping on a drum.

A golden drum full of air,
million bubbles we put in there,
the fucking magic of wheat,
never thinking for a minute.

"Ain't rose one fuckin' inch this, pal. Fuckin' bin the fuckin' lot."

"We shouldn't've bothered with that rotten yeast."

"We – you fuckin' put it in you dozy cunt!"

"Aye, well, we'd nothing else... Are you ready for another can? I'm
having a swift brandy before I get down to them scones."

"I'll stick on cans, me heart's burning."

One by one we turn out the dozen, one by one they line up on the rack, wasted wheat and heat and effort.

That's how many we'll shove in the bin, at four o'clock day after tomorrow.

Might shift odd 'un tomorrow as yesterday's bread, but it'll be an unlucky bastard who's unlucky enough to buy one even at that rate.

Some families lived on yesterday's bread.

"You can finish up them scones if you like."

No thanks mate. I've looked in that bowl and seen what you've done with your boiling hot fucking hands. Them scones are already fucked with two ingredients in the bowl.

"You knock yourself out, these Victoria sponge won't make their selves."

But near enough. If you know what you're doing.

Eight ounce times four, eggs, caster, self-raising, marge.
Teaspoon of baking powder. Mix that lot.
Pour it in tins.
Bake 'em.
Cool 'em, jam 'em.
Cream if you got it, if you're doing cream,
but you need a refrigerated cabinet, which we used to have,
but don't, now, dust 'em with sugar. Slice 'em up and sell 'em.
Piece of piss.

Right. Eggs.

"Where's the eggs?"

"Next you."

Tipping cottage fucking cheese out of a milk carton into them scones. Smell that from here. Fridge is fucked. Got to have some fucker out.

"That's empty, I beat last of them up to brush on them scones."

"Look in the fridge."

Eggs don't need go in the fridge, drives me up the fucking wall. Keep their selves fresh long before we rolled up, it's bloody nature.

And there's none in there any road.
But there's a fucking great mushroom, or something like,
making itself at home in the top corner.

Bloody ripe in there an' all. That's definitely been fucked longer than we think.
There's always flapjacks.
Everyone likes a flapjack, that's why they're everywhere. People reckon they're healthy and don't feel half as guilty is half the job, I reckon.

All they see is oats and think of porridge,
not the shitload of syrup and butter.
I'll do a dozen flapjacks.

"Were's the butter?"

"That's last what I've put in these."

Or marge. Marge'll do. Rancid marge.

And it feels like you get more for your money. They're heavy.
You don't, everything in 'em is dirt cheap,
but it's a proper chew so it feels like more for your money.

Don't bother with pre-packed shite though.
Got that fat in 'em that never goes off.
It blocks sewers and sits inside you for years and years.

Flapjacks even easier than Victoria sponge,
especially when you've no fucking eggs.

"I think your Dundee cake is burning."

"Take the fucker out then."

"Yeah, ohhh, I'm back on the brandy now. You?"

"Pour us one."

"Where's your glass?"

"That mug'll do."

"Something in it."

"Brandy?"

"Smells like piss."

Well we all have to go in a cup sometimes, I know I do,
then you forget and have a swig. So hit lucky this time.

"Give it a rinse, under the hot."

Used to shift shitloads of flapjacks, mostly them with one half dipped
in chocolate. Proper chocolate too, we used. Baking chocolate's alright
for going into stuff but not right to put neat in your gob.

Doesn't feel right. Powdery.

Don't need be fucking Cadbury's Milk or whatever,
so only costs a few pennies per batch more,
but the gaffer taught us never to cut a corner, not one,
because you never know why people come back.

It might be stuff you never think of.
It might be one single fucking thing you do well.

I've known shithouse bakeries scrape a living for years on just
one thing they done well, kept people coming back for more.

That's why we never shifted many Bakewell tarts.
Corner Bakery at the bottom there had that market fucking tied off,
don't waste your puff. If you wanted a Bakewell you went there. Even
I fucking went there, never said nothing, but they were bloody good.

Gaffer never sussed what they were doing to make their frangipane so
light, near drove himself round the fucking twist trying to work it out.

Gone now, Corner Bakery. Went to one of them We Buy Gold lot for
a bit, then one of them vapes. Then a different vapes. Then nothing.

Whole row gone last time I walked that way. Levelled.

If the Gaffer could see the corners we cut now he'd sit down and cry, but he can't, so is just as well...

"There's no hot coming through here."

Not the fucking boiler an' all.

"Just give it a good fucking wipe then."

"And the brandy be a bit antiseptic."

It tastes more like Dettol than brandy I'll give him that,
but at that price you might as well.
Brandy's brandy and for a fiver ain't bad.

"Them scones ain't turned out half bad you know."

"They look alright but there won't be no air in 'em.
Your crumb was greasy."

"They look alright though."

That's the egg wash. Multitude of sins under a carpet of pure gold.
Milk does alright, not bad, but them scones are shining like conkers.
I'd eat one, if I didn't know it'd be like a gobful of sweet fucking clay.

"And them are the sort of cake old ladies get and don't eat 'til they get sat down, 'cause they want to jam it up anyhow."

"Yeah."

"They won't bring it back once they've put it on a plate and sat down with a brew."

"If you say so."

"Once they're settled by their little fire is a long way for 'em to come back, they'll just eat it."

What the fuck are you on about now you shitfaced cunt?
Get this off him half the time now.
Winds his self up and he'll start crying in a minute.

"I never knew my grannies, me."

Tears.

"They wasn't dead, the cunts, nah, they didn't want fuck all to do with us. My brother was a fuckin' bastard."

Can't be fucking arsed with this.

"Get 'em out in the shop we got to get opened up, is gone eight."

"He fuckin' drowned in a reservoir in a nicked canoe."

I never fucking knew that. Knew he had a brother, but never said a word. Probably bullshit.

Is that smoke? Something burning. My fucking Dundee is burning.

"You left my fucking Dundee in you prick!"

"Don't blame me mate."

I ain't your fucking mate! I ain't –

Ahhh, that ain't too bad. Bit black round the edges but not bad,
not for me, I like the flavour of burnt almonds.
Bitter.
Most people don't. Too bitter. Which is bollocks.
Course they're too bitter if you pick 'em off and eat 'em on their own,

they're burnt, what do you fucking expect?

You take a bite of cake along with 'em and get the contrast.
Sweet fruit and cake, charred crust and burnt nuts,
all together at once in your mouth.

But will they?
No, nobody wants to take the rough with the smooth no more.
Every fucker wants smooth and nothing else.
Smooth and sweet.
They've forgot one makes the other.
They just look and see the charred bits and scorched nuts and say
fuck that burnt shite I'll get an iced finger.

A nice soft iced finger.
We should start doing iced fingers again. Why did we stop?
They are a piece of piss.

"Them scones are going to go I bet."

"Why'd we stop doing iced fingers?"

"Have we? Why?"

"I dunno, they're a piece of piss."

"You have to get the bread just right though."

"I can still make fucking sweet bread, pal!"

"Don't want it too sweet though."

You cheeky fucking bastard.

Ounce and a quarter caster sugar every pound of strong white flour,
that's all you need to know.

Neck on the cunt! Starting out I must've spent a fucking year
making four dozen of the fuckers every day!

Tell you what, it was a tray of my own made iced fingers
what I put in my wife's hands the day I met her!

Not more than two hundred yard from this shop.
Step out the door, turn right, then second left, keep walking, then
right again.
Mersey Street, the long one with the old mill at the top.
Was then. Torn down now. Little orange houses.
Only just closed its doors a few month back then.
Nobody on that street had a pot to piss in 'cos they all worked there,
generations of 'em.
Me and the gaffer done that walk a hot bright summer morning more
than 30 year ago.

Tray of iced fingers and a tray of scones and some sausage rolls
and odds and bits from the day before we was carrying.

They'd been round on the cadge for stuff for their street party they
was doing for one of the Royal things...

Wasn't one of their weddings, I do remember that...

And she wasn't the missus.
Just a girl at a street party,
wrestling with deckchairs,
trestle tables and paper plates,
fucking about with union jacks,
kids dashing excited,
in the sunshine,
under her feet.
Red mouth.
White blouse.
Blue eyes.

Brown arms.
Black hair.

Gaffer sneaks up, gives us a big fucking nudge in the ribs when I
hands over the stuff and goes 'if you're looking for a young fella this
lad makes best iced fingers in town, love, let him take you out you'll
never go to bed hungry'.

Or near enough that.

It was 30 year ago.
More.
Slept a lot since then.
Lot of things have come and gone.
More gone than come.

And then a big wink, cheeky old get,
and my face goes the colour of her lips.

Still it worked, it did, cos she wouldn't let us leave until we'd promised
to come back when the shop shut.

Closed early and I was away home and running,
gaffer laughing and shouting after us to change me undies
and then running back down Mersey Street
half-hour later, by then full of everyone laughing
and joking and playing music, by then,
my hair still wet from a stand-up wash,
and bits of bloody bog-roll plugging holes
up my neck and chin.
All the food had gone but I wasn't hungry and I found her and we had
a dance, then another, and we nattered away,
until it went dark,
and shared a Party 7,
she had a glass any road,
and slipped off to the park,
laughing and stopping and snogging all the way.

Heard next day that cunt turned up shitfaced chucking out time and
started swearing and getting into the Pakistani family, fighting with
the dad, so I heard, off of fucking him, proud of his self.

I didn't much care. Hadn't much slept. Away with the fairies.
Wasn't home 'til gone three in the morning and a 5am start.
Head up me arse and over the moon I was.

The Jubilee.
It was the Jubilee, if you remember that.
They made a big fuss. There was a silver bus.
They came round asking for that wedding couple of year ago
and I made a few bits, took 'em over, but it wasn't nowhere the same.

Handful of people, all old. Two little tables.
What kids there was was watching and teasing.
I dropped off the bits and come back here.

Rained an' all.

"I'm opening another brandy, then going through the front."

"Make a change from going through at the back."

"Eh?"

"Top us off, I'll knock them trifles up."

"And the jam tarts."

"I never said them."

"Thought you had."

"I was thinking about 'em but I didn't say nothing."

"You know what you should do with that Dundee cake?"

"Fuckin' smash it on the floor?"

"Ha ha ha ha. Marzipan it up like a Simnel Cake."

"That's..."

Probably worth a go.
Roll a sheet nice and thin, drop it over the top, score with a fork,
brush on some let-down apricot jam, under an hot grill.
Look good that, like it was done on purpose.

"Take the fucking nuts off first though, nobody wants burned nuts.
Taste bitter as fuck."

Fucking piss off you can't taste nothing any road.
You've drunk rubbing alcohol and said it'd be alright with tonic,
your tongue is dead.
It wouldn't have done neither. Better in a shitload of Coke.

And there won't be no trifles neither. How can there be trifles with the fridge gone to fuck? No fridge, no jelly. Milk's gone west so no custard. No cream.

A pair of stale lardy Victoria sponge ain't a trifle!
Jelly never get set now anyhow.
Should have had that in first thing with the sponge soaking.

In the fucked fridge,
with the warm specials,
and the mushroom.
No bits of fruit,
no fucking bananas,
dash of sherry,
if we had any sherry.

I like a sherry.
Shame, because trifles used to go.
Old ladies, most, they like the fussy stuff.
Bulk of the dainty cakes are for the old ladies.

Battenberg, that's the old ladies.
That's why that Mr Kipling advert about having a whole one to yourself used to kill me.
No you cunt that wasn't everyone's dream! That was the old ladies' dream, no fucker else ever had that dream. All them have.

It's the Royal thing, they all love that, the women. They're more romantic.
Most of 'em. Plenty not give a fuck.

They was the only ones turned out for that last wedding though,
I know that, sat in the street with little flags,
and someone young and bored there having a fag,
waiting push 'em home.

Battenberg first got invented special for one of the Royals,
is what it is, back when that was their name, before the first war,
when nobody cared or could do fuck all about it any road.

They'll have had recipes out the Woman's Realm or down the WI.
Ever since all the grannies and mums will have thought it something
special, I reckon, a little slice of the Royal life.

Only a few ounce though, because it was dearer than a scone or a Jap
or what you like. Light and delicate we made ours, lovely light sponge
the Gaffer, like a cloud in your mouth.
A pretty slice, an' all, wrapped up tight in white tissue paper.

Was the only one got put in the bread tissue, Battenberg, I think.
Fall apart if you shove it in a bag.

Only jam and thin rolled marzipan hold the cunt in one piece!
Shove a skint old girl's 2oz sliver of Battenberg in a bag and
she'd have a bag of squares and a hoop by time she sat down.

Alice and the girls always folded the tissue just so,
nice and tight and stiff, with the corners tucked in,
a little shining parcel in the old ladies' hands,
and I sometimes thought of 'em unwrapping it at home,
thinking it something special, eating it slow.

I still see that.

Some blokes had a slice, now and then,
a thick slice, but you always looked at them a bit funny,
for the laugh, done an 'I'm free', back then anyway.
People just did, we wasn't nasty.

So did their mates, you were only joining in. Is only a bit of fucking
cake, who gives a shit? And I didn't mind a slice, every now and then.
Not regular.

But that prick called one bloke a puff and said he had AIDS and got
fucking sparked out for his trouble.

And I had the odd slice, with a hot tea.
I like anything with a bit of marzipan.

There are almond people and I'm one.
I'll nibble a bit of marzipan doing this...

People forget you had to weigh it.

"We're open y'know, I'm on me fucking tod if it gets busy.
Is something fuckin' burnin'?"

"When did I put them flapjacks in?"

"You fuckin' put 'em in."

"Fuckin' bollocks!"

Never burned a thing, once.
We had a clock but after a few year you don't need it.
Few years in the flour you have headful of clocks,
all ticking toward different bells,
and you with a close eye on 'em all.
Pork pies out in five,
knock it down a notch,

scones in once it's down,
then white barm out,
brown cob ten to go,
and so on, tick, tick, tick...

Gets harder to keep track though, along the line.

Time changes on you, gentle, and you never really notice,
you catch on to it too late, when you're already fucked,
 if you're in a job where time is half the job.

I reckon what it is is, you get so there's more of it behind you than ahead,
and the small bit ahead is harder to see,
because it's small,
so you look back more and that feels eas-

"FUCKING BASTARD!"

"Ha ha ha haaaa!"

"Fuck that was hot!"

"Been in oven y'daft cunt, what'd you expect?"

Fuck that was hot.
Not worst burn I've had mind. Not worst this week. Keep grabbing hot trays all the time now, always not thinking, smelling smoke and rushing about.

"Ha ha haaah! Fuckin' mutterin' away to yourself!"

"Fuck off and get us some butter you cunt."

"You should have used a cloth."

"No, fuckin' really? Butter, butter!"

Butter for burns.
Always, good blast under the cold tap then butter.
He knows, that cunt.
Took a tea loaf out bare-handed other week,
so fucked he held the tin for two minute talking shit
and peeled both his palms down to bare meat.

I laughed my fucking tits off.
So did he.
Until he smashed his Bells half hour later
because his hands was all buttered.

"There's only margarine left – here let us tip brandy on 'em..."

"Get the fuck off with that!"

At least bad marge don't smell much, not like rancid butter.
So there's that.

Who's going want to eat them fucking flapjacks?
You could strike a match on the dried-out bastards.
Look like they'd cut your fucking mouth.

Fucking would cut your mouth.
Oats bake rock hard, them corners'd slash up the roof of your gob
piece of piss, no bother.

"Have we any chocolate, slap over this fuckin' lot?"

"What you asking me for?"

"I..."

What the fuck am I asking him for? Nothing ever comes back from

that cunt except questions and bollocks.
I'm a one man band since they carried the gaffer out of here.

If I don't know no fucker knows, and I don't know a fucking... clue.

"Are you ready for brandy?"

"Top us off."

"Where's your mug?"

"You're fuckin' holding it."

"I've had a piss in that before, you sure?"

"When?"

"Er..."

"Top us off and get in the fuckin' shop, some fucker'll be robbin' us blind."

"Fuck off arsehole. Say when..."

"To the top. When."

Chocolate's in the cupboard with the dried fruit, where the peel,
the chopped nuts, the angelica, the dessicated coconut,
all that stuff is, if we got any.

Reminds me. Marzipan. Apricot jam.
Just mix a spoon of that in two spoons of warm water then brush it on.
Fork it up first.

Makes crunchy bits.

Apricot brandy used to be nice, enjoyed that.
Apricots are something to do with almonds. In nature...

A glass or two Christmas Day, after dinner, little 'un crawling about
with a box on her head and the missus pulling her hair out because
her dad's pissed and making a prick of his self as usual.

One year, dancing, daft twat shoved his arm through the glass of a
display cabinet.
Spent afternoon in casualty.
On his fucking Jones though, we watched James Bond.

Always a good-natured drunk though, as I saw, never a cunt on it,
not that I saw, we got on, as it went, but a drinker, and not just
Christmas.

And then, she reckoned he had been a cunt,
any road, a few times, enough times,
when she was little.

Pissed all their money away,
either way,
growing up. Put years on her mother.

She shuffled off in her 50s. Not much about her, I never thought.
She fell down stairs more than once so that'll have took it out of her,
it will though won't it?

Fuck knows what happened to him.

No chocolate? You have to be fucking joking.
We should have. Fuck me we should have or what are we doing?

Time was we had a walk-in cupboard full of all that, full of everything.

Needed a ladder to reach the top,

everything you always needed,
always fresh and to hand,
everything you need, full stop.

Couldn't be in there longer than a minute!
Hum off all that fruit, always a few hundredweight each of sultanas,
currents, raisins, was nice at first but knocked me sick if I hung about.

Nothing ran out, never, the Gaffer ran stock like a hawk. Chocolate
is fucking basic. Fucking tons of cakes out the fucking window when
you can't put your hands on some piss-arsed chocolate.

Chocolate cake.
Chocolate eclair.
Florentine.
Oh aye, Florentine...
how long has that been?
What a treat, what a fucking treat they are.

My missus loved my Florentine.
Ate 'em over a plate,
up under her chin,
never wasting a crumb,
not fucking one,
hoovered 'em up with her finger.

Purring she'd be, eyes half open, first bite to last morsel.

Got me out of jail rolling home any bloody state if I'd a couple of them
in my bag, for a few year any road.

They was fucking good though.
Only good goes in 'em, the way we done 'em, don't it?
No bulk to 'em, just a bit, but pure good stuff, bit of flour aside.

Glacé cherries, candied peel,

almonds, butter,
golden syrup and walnuts,
soft brown sugar,
dark chocolate.
Pure good stuff, just a bit of flour, a bit to do a job.
Few ounce to bind the good stuff together,
only the best stuff go in 'em,
and when you got the bastards just right...

And the gaffer had got the bastards just right,
so we got 'em right in our turn,
our Florentine was his Florentine,
at his shoulder learned,
then him at our shoulder,
barking and taking the piss,
but giving a toss,
taking the time to see we saw,
and did as he done.

'There's no cherries in that one you soft bugger!'
Never done many, small batches, and then only certain days.
They come out too pricey for round here as a rule,
too dear by half really, even when everything was going alright.

That much good stuff costs,
and when the factory went,
when all the factories went,
and you could get two scones for the same,
or a vanilla slice and change,
or two fat slices of Madeira,
well you have to, haven't you?

Can't always have the treats you want,
make do with treats you can get.

For weekends only, and less and less, over time.

Put 'em out Friday, they'd be good until Saturday if you keep them
cool and dry. Never made many at a time and we always sold more or
less what we made, so we had it about right.

A good few coming to Christmas, and you could order 'em,
with your cake or mince pies, half dozen or a dozen,
and people did, and Alice and the girls will do the dozen up
in a nice red cardboard box for you.

Sixes come in a bag. The boxes cost a bit.

Be five years since done a batch. Knocking 'em out at that big ADLD
on the park off the bypass for a quarter what we can do 'em at in here.

Like everything, they're not as good, they're a stab at it.
Shit chocolate, be full of hydrogenated shit, not butter,
but they cost less, and tick the same box in your head,
so no point us wasting our fucking time, is there?

We can only do what sells.
What we can leave out longest.
What we can afford to waste.
Christ I only need a few bloody ounce, to melt, half a bar!
Cooking chocolate will do, sorry gaffer, for this,
quick dip of the top and they'll look fair enough at the quid.

Plenty of paper bun cases, plenty of them.
Small muffin cases it says on the tube.
Used to be buns, just buns, they're muffins now.
Or cupcakes.

Fuck off with cupcakes and muffins, it's buns.

Muffins are soft rolls for toasting,
made to split with your hands and tear,
for hundreds of fucking year,

like I got shown to fucking make before all this shit.
And cupcakes are baby food for grown-ups.
He keeps reckoning we should do 'em but never, in here.
Over my dead body, in here.

There's fucking nothing in here. Bag there with six fucking raisins in
it and them long gone. Why put that back on the shelf? Dickhead.

Maybe I done it. I'd eat them if they wasn't fucking gone. Was always
slipping in the back for a sneaky peck at the raisins.

Gaffer never minded so long as you didn't take the piss. He was at
'em too, is thing, swore by 'em. Told me there was nothing better for
keeping regular, and he wasn't wrong.

At one time I shit like a clock. Don't need any help with that any more,
though. Other way about really.

He was fit as a fiddle.
In here before five every morning until gone 70.
Strong as fuck from humping flour and
kneading life into a million loaves.

That's how come when he had his stroke, a fucking whopper, it didn't
kill him. Should have.

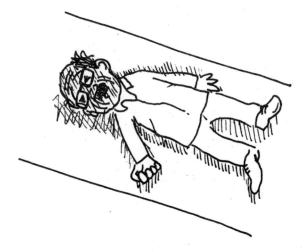

But it just laid him out, out there, in the shop, behind the counter,
where we stand, Christmas Eve 1990-something.

He was locking up, we'd all pissed off the pub.

Lay there most the night an' all, Alice thought he was having a pint with
us, me and that cunt, for Christmas. We always tried to, back then.

He was meant to too, but he didn't, and we'd thought he'd couldn't
been arsed in the end.

Gone straight home to Alice and spent a quiet night with her,
just the pair of 'em in that big house.

There's lots of candles.
Should be with the numbers, these.

Bags of candles, pink and blue...

Soon

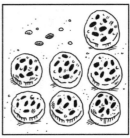

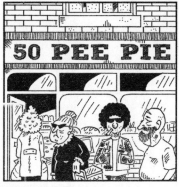

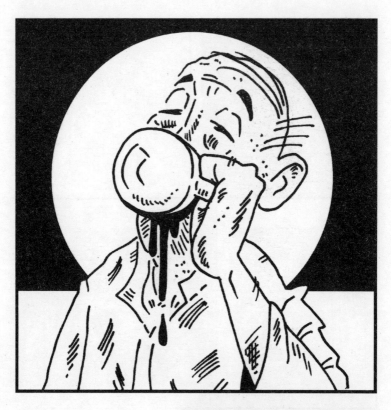

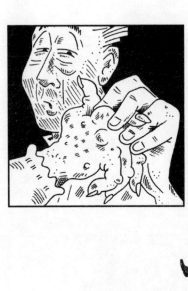

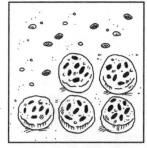

"What was you dreaming?"

I never done that. I never done nothing like that.
Only person I've ever hit is that cunt.

"No fuckin' idea. How long was I kippin'?"

"Fuck knows, hour or two."

"What time we at?"

"You was laughing your fuckin' head off, scared the shit out of that
old woman."

I've never even ever seen her with a bruise on her so that's a load
of bollocks.
You remember something like that, wouldn't you? Your dreams play
tricks don't they? See all sort of shit you've never done but you think
you did when you wake up, for a bit.

"Frigging about an' all. She jumped and dropped all her coppers,
silly old cow."

"There was music playing, I was dancing with someone."

"Fuckin' chasin' pennies round the floor for an hour,
while you sit there pissin' and groaning shit."

"What shit?"

"Rubbish, shit. Blehh blehh blehh... Scared her enough."

She never had no cause for complaints there. Whatever else it's never
taken me that way. Makes me happy, most, did then any road. So long
as I take it easy on the scotch, but everyone's that way on the scotch,
it's fucking mad.

Scotch makes me angry,
beer makes me sleep,
brandy makes you randy,
gin makes us weep.
Same as for everyone whisky, that though, ain't it?
Made of soil for fuck's sake.
Everything else just makes me knackered now.

"I'm lucky, I don't ever dream any more, I just wake up and I've been asleep."

"Is the clock right?"

"Most times is like I blink, and it's gone from day to night like that."

"It ain't fuckin' tickin'."

"Like that."

"Like what?"

"I can't snap me fingers no more..."

Can't hear the bastard ticking but can't remember right if it's the sort that does tick or not but I'm sure it's said just gone two too long now.

We've had it years an' all. It does fucking tick, it drives me up the fucking wall, ticking. Or is that the big one in the back?

"I don't ever feel like I've had no rest mind..."

"When'd you last change the battery?"

"Ohh, no, I've never done that, me."

"Stopped ain't it?"

"Dunno, am fairly sure wasn't then when I looked before."

"When was that?"

"Now you're asking... I think I've been asleep a bit too."

We need to know the fucking time.
We need to know when we can lock up, cash up and get the fuck away from him. Bet this is why we keep burning stuff.

"What happened to your brother in the end?"

"Eh?"

"Your Adam."

"Adrian. He fuckin' died years back."

"Oh aye he did. I remember seeing you cry now, when that letter come. He was a lovely bloke..."

"You never fuckin' well met him."

"I did, he come in here one day."

"He'd got wed and moved half round the fuckin' world before you'd hardly fuckin' started."

"Well who was that that I seen in here that time?"

"I got no idea."

"Who was that I seen you with in that pub garden that time?"

"That was me Dad."

"Ahhh, I knew you was the younger one. How's he getting on?"

"He's fuckin' dead an' all."

Shifted another pair of slice of Dundee while I was off that's good.
That's close half a cake sold there, that's alright that.
Bob or two up on it already with another few day to sell as fresh to go.

Looks nice that marzipan, do that again. Got to get more marzipan.
And everything, the cupboard's fucking bare.

"You look like your dad."

"Aye, people said that."

"Did I ever meet him?"

"You seen him, then."

"What's he up to now?"

"He's fuckin' dead I said."

Dead a fair while an' all. Both are. Mum more, she were young. Quiet bloke. Hard worker. Lorry driver. Never hit us, Mum took care of that, and fuck me she knew how to sting your arse if you was fucking about.

He never said much. Never round much. Always away, he done the trunks. Couple of days a week home, and spent half that in his shed or a pair of legs sticking out from under the car. Mum looked to us two, mostly.

He was alright though. A quiet bloke who worked hard.
And not one for the drink, that I ever saw, but he had a drink, like all of us.
Kept driving a good few year after Mum went, and me and the Missus moved into the house, because she was expecting, and Dad was still only home two day a week, and our flat was shit.

Soon as he retired he told us he was away to Dumfries because there was a lady there he'd met, and known a while, and she was the widow of a friend of his from driving.

He was worried I'd think he was doing wrong by Mum, I told him not to worry.
She'd been gone a long while.
Why be lonely when you don't need?

That's what I told him.

Never met her, but I'd met her husband because me and Adrian went in the lorry, a bit, to places, and he drove out of the company's Scottish depot.

Never went nowhere any good, exciting or beautiful or anything.
Middlesbrough once, Hamilton a few times. Parked on the racecourse there had fish and chips.

But the journey was the thing, hammering along like King of the Road.

Gordon something, he was.
A jack give out and a lorry cab come down on half of him.
Survived a few day, Dad went up and seen him in the hospital.
Said his whole body was a bleeding bruise.
He was a nice bloke, I remember.

Dad and her never wed, but the funeral was up there.
I couldn't get, with this place.

"My dad was a right cunt, looked fuck all like me."

"Who took them other slices of Dundee then?"

"That little thin bald lass with the dog she ties up."

"The yappy little bastard?"

"Back legs a pair of wheels."

"I think I know who y'mean..."

"She used to come in here when I started here, me, her, and I tell you what – she was bonny an' all."

"Don't remember her."

"You weah... All fuckin' gone now like."

Should have a slice of that Dundee before much else of anything to drink. Raw brandy on empty guts can't do so much as I used to, fucking burn like Hell these days.

And nothing's gone in there since –

"What did I eat before?"

"When?"

"Today."

"I had a flapjack, me. Not bad neither. Bit hard but I don't mind a chew."

"I had something, after I was sick."

"When was you sick?"

"Before."

"You was sick yesterday."

Was that yesterday? Yeah, it was an' all.
Slice of that'll go alright then, fill us out a bit.
Three slice left to sell and already up on it.

Looks right enough. Bad marge right off, but I know, they don't.
We'll get away with it. Marmalade masks it, nobody will know unless they're looking.
Just in the background. You know when you taste bad even though you can't really taste it, but just know it's there, hanging over everything?

That's this.

"I'll open another brandy eh?"

"How many've we had?"

"This'll make five. It's not so strong..."

Tastes strong enough here. Goes down like battery acid.

Must take a bottle home, he will and it comes out of the pot after all.

Never get my half any road.
Never gets nothing of his own, does all his drinking on me. Bet he's already stashed a bottle or two away somewhere for home time the sneaky fucker.

I fucking know I have.

"My dad's dead an' all, and fuckin' longer ago than yours was."

"I know."

"I was so young I didn't understand what the funeral was, but I remember it like it was last week."

"You said the same the other day."

"Did I?"

"Yeah, you said you thought it meant he was coming back because your mum was so happy."

Easy done though. See that when you get older, you do less,
you've only a few memories worth saying out loud, less worth listening to, and you forget when you've told your few stories, or who was listening.

I'm as bad. I'm as bad.
Only knew my little 'un six and a bit years, and most of that me grafting in here, then out a lot of the nights, and time flies and they'd gone away before I had a chance to do any different.

So only have a few stories,
you read 'em over again,
growing, changing,

but always the bloody same.

Starting to bore myself with 'em fuck knows what that cunt thinks.
Not I give a fuck what that cunt thinks. He's the same.
Ain't listening to me no more than I listen to him, half the time.

We're not friends, never have been. He's my business partner, that's all.

Fucking hell.

"She was dancing when we got to the do,
and give us a sip on her Babycham and brandy."

"Nice drink that, my missus had that a bit."

"We can get Babycham for this, they brought it back…"

"Perry ain't it?"

"Think my dad was a bit of a cunt with her all told."

"There's a lot of 'em about."

"All I remember about the cunt is his feet, bit odd that ain't it?"

"Big fuckin' feet, he was a right big fucker, black leather slip-ons, buckles like The Sweeney. All I see is him stamping and shouting."

Couldn't give a fuck. Just want to get up that fucking hill and home.

"Stamped all over a lantern I made 'cos I bust his good knife on the turnip."

"And hit your mum, I know."

"I'm older than he ever got to though, so that's fuckin' something."

"Yeah..."

"Cancer. Fags the cunt. Always one on."

"You opening that brandy or telling me your life story again?"

Happy about that Dundee cake. Not bad, sweet and dark and bitter and crumbly, like is meant to be. Like the Gaffer's or mum's.

They'd never have used bad marge like, sooner not bother.
Sat a bit heavy on us, an' all, but there's no grief.
Taste it on belches. Not sickly or nothing, just sharp, and off.

It's this brandy.

"Say when."

Fuck do I shake like that?

"When."

"Oops."

"When y'dickhead."

"Fuckin'... bollocks..."

He's had more than any two bottle that crafty bastard. Like a jelly trying keep that bottle straight, look at state, slopping it all over.

Face half hanging off him.

He'll have been sneaking away for the odd crafty, that's his style.
Mind you, did we have some beer an' all?
We must have for me to let go in my sleep, so that'll have helped.
I am feeling it.

He's been sneaking for a sly swig of something tucked away since day he walked in here that fucker.
A sneaky here,
a sneaky there,
a sneaky fuckin' everywhere.

Biked it back then. Him on a fucking bike! With his bike bottles full of shorts.

Scooting out back every ten minute.
Rolling come afternoon and I reckon the Gaffer knew,
but he never pulled him up on it.
He got through the work pissed or not, back then,
so you know, you're a man aren't you?

Make your own mistakes then live with 'em.

Once I'd twigged his bike booze I started having a sneaky swig on 'em an' all, just wait for him to slide off then go soon as he got back, while he's busy trying to look busy.
Nice little laugh when I seen his cunty face later on wondering how he's necked it so quick.

I always liked a drink but hardly never brung it in here, and never more than odd quarter or half, never, to keep us going, odd times.
Some of them deep winter mornings.
But always done my drinking either at home or on the way home, most of it, from respect for the Gaffer.
He never respected him, fucking used him. Him and Alice.
Borrowed off 'em for his bit of this shithole, know that.

Not that the Gaffer didn't enjoy a drink.
Bitter and scotch he'd stick it away forever and never show fuck all except he turned bright fucking red. Proper red. Like a red on a snooker table.

The Gaffer liked a drink,
fucking loved a drink,
must have seen him sink
ten thousand handfuls,
him and Alice liked a drink.

Most Saturdays he'd stand anyone in the shop who fancied it three or four come knocking off, and I usually did, down the church club, which was even cheaper than the pubs.

Missus come down to meet up,
before the kid, if able,
and we'd have a day of it,
one big happy table,
the lasses out front,
the Gaffer, Alice,
and that cunt.

That was long before the little 'un come along, when we was in the flat, so we'd stop out for the night, have a bar snack, but she wasn't much of a drinker. She liked a drink like we all like a drink, but I never seen her drunk.
Not pissed. Tipsy never shitfaced.

Most likely be down to the way her dad was, I've always thought.
Put her off the heavy stuff.

She'd take a port and lemon
or an half of lager and lime,
or a brandy and Babycham,
getting toward closing time.
One day that cunt come rolling off his bike on the way home and
smashed fuck out of his face on them iron railings round the station.

Got 'Panda' off me and the Gaffer for fucking weeks but when one of
the lasses said it he went fucking mental.
And walked in every day with his bike even though the fucker
couldn't ride it because the wheel was buckled. Bottles, see.

The bike only went once the Gaffer finished.
Disappeared first day after, first day back in after that Christmas,
walks in with two carrier bag of all sorts he said was leftover from
Christmas, and we had right good few days on it to be fair.

Brung my Christmas leftovers in when they'd gone.
When they'd gone we nipped the selling-out shop and bought some
in and there we was, just normal then.

And they were busy days, with the Gaffer in hospital and just the two lasses out the front then, because Alice had gone.
Her hands was all knotted up and they hurt her.
That bog-eyed lass, what was her name?

"What was that bog-eyed girl out front here round when Gaffer went down with his stroke?"

"Florence. Liked me her."

"Fuck off, she was no more than 20."

"We had it off a good few time."

"Get to fuck, she was going out with that drippy lad,
used to come and pick her up."

"Few Saturdays when she was pissed, round back of the church, honest."

"She was a bit simple that lass."

"Ha ha, aye, she was nothing much to look at neither."

"They got wed them two."

Me and him made their wedding cake. He done all the decorations.

"I pissed in their wedding cake!"

"Nasty bastard."

"Only a little fuckin bit in the icing. I think it were theirs…"

Just paid for materials, like me and the missus, that's all we paid,
for the fruit mostly, that's where all the cost is really,

like when me and the Gaffer made my wedding cake, before that.

Then she left, got wed, moved away.
He'd got himself something better somewhere miles away.

Then there was me, and him, and Carole, and she was always knackered with that lad of hers.

"I'm not liking this brandy much any more."

"You won't, it's shite."

Not that it was getting as busy by then.
We'd already had first of them Greggs bastards pop up hadn't we, and a new big supermarket in the old mill there, knocking out the crusty baguettes for next to nothing.

Shit they were an' all, fuck all like French bread. I'd had the proper stuff, in France on a trip, these was just the shape dickheads seen on the fucking telly, Pink Panther and that, nothing else...

Still shit an' all, the basic ones you get, unless you're happy to spend out on their fucking Extra Best or Simply The fucking Taste, whatever.
Just fucking gum they are, with a soppy fucking crust on 'em.
But people like something new don't they? And get carried away.
Should have had a stab here but thought they was a fucking fad,
like them fucking cupcakes, are a fad now.
The bread wasn't but them fucking cakes are. Baby food they are.

Carole went not long after, saved us letting her go,
and she was last help we had.
Just me and that cunt since then.

"Don't tell me you nobbed Carole an' all."

"Who?"

"Older lass was the last out front here."

"Her with the dickhead kid?"

"He had that autism though didn't he, that lad?"

"He had summat, come in here once or twice,
wailin' and wavin' his fuckin' arms about,
made a right cunt of his self."

"Poor little bastard, wasn't him to blame."

"He weren't that fuckin' little, big six foot solid get when I seen him.
He'd have took some knockin' out."

"He'll be in his 40s or about now."

"She's fuckin' dead though."

"Is she?"

"Yeah."

"How?"

"Stopped breathing, ha ha ha!
Fuck knows, I just heard."

Always looked buggered.
Wonder who takes care of that lad now. That man, as he'll be.
I know the dad fucked off years ago, miles before she was on here.
Down to the kid, I expect.
Some people aren't cut out for it are they?
Ain't many saints. Be fuckin' horrible, if you think.
Everyone reckons they would, but I'd like to see them all try.

Just them two together all them years.

"She had a big black eye that once didn't she?"

"Who had?"

What's he fucking on about? Never told him that, I just said I was dancing with Alice. Drink never took me that way, not then, not at all.

"Her, Carole, who'd you fuckin' think? He was a big solid cunt that fucker."

"Wonder who looks after him now."

"A fuckin' loony bin I hope."

"They ain't got them no more, they leave them to take their own medicine."

Maybe he killed her. You hear about that. Nah, we would have heard about that. Maybe done herself. Don't make such a fuss of them these days.

"Oh aye, they shut the Moor."

"Thousands up in the Moor one time. My grandad done a stint in the laundry up there when he come out of the war."

"They shut the Moor just after my Mum went in. Do you want a topper?"

"A little splash."

Was its own little town to itself up there, everything you need.
Shops, football pitches, tennis, cricket.
Fucking great social club they had up there an' all,

three full-size snooker, pool, darts. You had to know someone, but I did.

Hundreds worked up the Moor.
Football and cricket teams won everything going. My grandad reckoned he only got on because he was a good footballer and handy at cricket an' all.

Proper ballroom out back of that social club, you went through a door and it all opened up, big high ceiling with a chandelier and a sprung floor, all wood for dancing.
Went a New Year do up there, 1980-somewhere, a big band and everything.
Alice and the gaffer babysat.
They done a lot, because we were still young.

They was always happy to take her, and she always come home wanting go back 'cos they'd made such a fuss. Spoiled her rotten, really. Fucking teddy bear bigger than she was one birthday and she run and hide. Never took to it.
Too big.

They didn't take it with them, anyway, so she can't have asked.
Or maybe there wasn't room in the car. It was only a Panda...

Should've gone and seen Alice, is what it is.
But she'd only have asked about her and how she was getting on and
say she'd love to see her, just once more, and start herself off crying.
And what do you say anyway when you haven't got a fucking clue?

All gone now. Pulled the lot down.

Bar the main building, that's swanky flats,
and umpteen hundred of them little orange houses they put up now,
all about it, covering the wings and the pitches and the laundry.

There was a good cheggy tree back in the woods behind the laundry
only me and Adrian knew about, I reckon. Buckets of conkers we
picked up.
You'd see the patients wandering about between the trees,
but they never minded us.

When they come to shut it up they said half of 'em should never
have been in there in the first place, but they always seemed happy
enough to me.

Probably a sight better off in there just their selves with each other
than out here with us fucking cunts.
Don't know what happened to the ballroom,
I'm sure it'll be something else now.

People don't dance the same, do they? I ain't danced in fucking years.

"This brandy is fuckin' wearin' me out I'm back on the cans, me."

I thought we'd had some beer.

"I'll have one, what is there?"

"Just Kestrel now."

Something lighter. That Dundee ain't sat right and this brandy ain't helping. Bad marge and brandy burning holes in us. Hernia haven't I? Felt shite months then boom, spewing in here four hour straight one day few year back with that cunt rolling about and me curled on the floor.

Ended up in an ambulance and a trolley on morphine in a corridor for half a fucking day and night.

Because of my lifestyle, the doctor said,
but I goes I don't have a lifestyle I just have a life,
and he said you have to drink less.

Shouldn't drink at all,
first thing they said,
knock that on the head,
red rag to a bull,
and they was right,
but you get used to it.

Get used to anything when it's been normal long enough don't you?
That's why ageing don't send everyone mad. It's all loss adjustment.

Used to be a bloke come in here with half his face gone from something,
but he was always laughing and joking, as I saw.

Maybe not when he's home alone looking into a mirror,
but nobody's laughing then are they?
Apart from proper fucking nutters.

You should have seen poor cunt trying to eat a hot pie.

Bitter'd do me fine at minute, settle us.

Never get bitter any more but I used to enjoy a bitter.
A middling bitter, none of that malty shite, a Boddies or thereabouts.

Used to be able to get a keg, two gallon keg, homebrew place along
there round the corner done 'em, under the counter, their own brew.
It was alright.
We'd be alright if we were just getting a couple of kegs in for the day.
Sweat it out easy. Calms your guts, bitter.
Best out of a pump though. Long while since had a pint out of a pump.

Boddies they had on Queen's Head was a lovely pint. Mother's milk,
that, slipped away, lift the glass to your mouth and breathe in.

Be 13p, my first there, never forget. Fucking hammered for a quid.
Sick as a dog at school next day.

"You're in luck."

"Oh aye, dead lucky me, a warm fuckin' Special."

"It's Tennents though..."

Stopped cheap for years.
Only about 15p by time I was on here full time.
Only on about £15 nicker a week, mind,
and bloody Mum had whipped five of that housekeeping before I'd
got my coat off Friday night.
Still about fifty pint over though, and a dance,
few trips the flicks, few bag of chips and fags.

"I ain't had a pint in a pub for ages."

"Can't even remember, me."

"Could go a pint of that Boddies they had on in the Queen's."

"They'd Gold Label Barley Wine tap in there."

"Fuckin' horrible."

"Aye but 10-odd percent, pint only about 5p more."

"Nah, nobody seemed think so much about strength back then."

"I fuckin' did. Boddies is gnat's piss."

"Done all my drinking in pubs once upon a while."

"Me an' all, but who's the money for that when there's all the fuckin' deals?"

He ain't wrong.

Don't ask for who
the Bells is half price,
it's half price for Halloween,
or Firework Night,
or –

Boozeland flogging two one litre vodka at twenty the other week.

Twenty. Fucking. Quid. Two litre.

We got four, at that price you're a mug n
one you see empty bottles of in the street

Red label. One man's name.

Always what they bootleg to knock
people blind in the local rag when
that happens.

Not the worst I've had, to be fair.
Not the blinding one, the proper one.

And who wants sit in a noisy pub full
of fucking people waiting on get served and then be slung out for fuck
all half the time when there's that right on your way home from work?

And that lad with the van,
goes here to Calais and back twice a month,
so you can get a week's bevvy out of that van for sixty quid.
How can your pubs match that?

I hope that don't dry up now they've fucked off out of Europe.
That'd be a ball-ache.

"Pubs are shite now any road."

"Too bright."

"Pictures of fuckin' cheese everywhere."

"Eh?"

"And they're all kids in 'em! No fuckin' old timers no more, not like
it was."

"Aye, there was more people our age now in when we was young..."

"They just don't go no more."

"Can't afford."

"And they're scared of getting battered."

"Aye, there's some rum cunts about."

"And full of fuckin' women!"

"There's always been a few women in –"

"How can they beat the fuckin' deals you get now?"

Swear to God there was a pub every few hundred steps,
whichever way you went this town once.

Felt like, any road. Queen's, Golden Cross, Fleece, Craven Heifer,
Withy Trees, I can't remember 'em all. Fair crowd every night in 'em
an' all, laughing and shouting and playing doms.

Might as well have, because thing is didn't used to be so much cheaper
to do your drinking outside the pubs than in 'em, selling-out shops
wasn't knocking it out for fuck-all back then.

They was more about getting hold of some to have in the house for
when you was at home than they was about saving money, back then.
Only got proper cheap when supermarkets started knocking it out for
fuck-all get fuckers through the door buy other stuff.

Cheap then, at least, to what it was in the pubs, by then,
which had got miles dearer, by then.

Done myself a favour,
was a liquor saver,
done myself a favour,
liquor saved in Kwik Save.

Next thing the Threshers and Unwins and them was going belly-up
and all the selling-outs went to Bargain Boozes and Booz&Noozes
and Boozelands and Booze Brothers and SuperBoozes and them.

"The fuckin' deals you get now!"

"Last pint I bought in a pub set us back near three quid, I know that."

"Three quid's a three litre Zeppelin, that, and it's fuckin' eight per cent! You get leathered for a day at home on the price of a round!"

"That Wetherspoons is a bit cheaper I've heard."

"Not so fuckin' much! Thirty quid easy if you're after drinking whole day in there I bet."

Put it in what was the old bank in the middle of town a few year ago, lovely building what'd fell to fuck and ruin since the TSB cleared out.

Done a nice job, to be fair, and been rammed when I've passed. Killed a few old boozers off round it, that, and now they're the ones dropping to bits.

The Durham Ox looks like you could shove it over.
Give and take though life, ain't it?
They was pegging out any road is the truth.
Half the old pubs already shut up shop by time that opened.

Windows boarded over after hundred years and more some.
Old England on the junction across from the nick been torn down, last time I passed. All stone that was, hundred-odd years that been there.

Triangle of sand and holes now, like it never happened at all.

Bridge Inn is flats full of fucking junkies staring out the window.
Mind you that was always a rough hole. Too near the station.
Built right into the last bridge before the platforms,
and used to shake like fuck when a big train come in or out.

Seen some lad glassed in there one night,
I kid you not I watched his eyeball roll half down his cheek.

The Blackamoor burned down.

Ten pub crawl any night,
any end of town,
another night after,
to different pubs,
that time around.

Friday nights always heavy, which was hard being in here on
Saturdays for four of a morning because then Saturdays was fucking
hard going, here.

Everyone after bread enough 'til Monday, and a big pie day, Saturday,
lads and blokes heading the pub or the match, and housewives
needing a little treat of a cake, a cream Victoria or such, in a white
box, cut up and put out for everyone Sunday afternoon.

So cop a Friday lock-in and you was home just long enough to piss
and drop your guts then you're back out the door down the road to
here, and the gaffer yelling 'Where the bloody hell have YOU been?'
louder than normal and slamming the tins extra hard and laughing,
because he knows you're fucking dying.

Saturdays were great though, none of that Sunday.
A proper hard knock, time flew you was grafting that hard,
working up a thirst, few pint with the gaffer and Alice, generally,
then home for a rinse and off round town opening time.
Bag of chips on the way then pub, pub, stretching your legs and night
air waking you up or sending you fucked every half hour, and a lock-
in if you ended up in the right boozer. Always loved a lock-in.
Felt special, like you was getting away with something, didn't it?

Landlord tips a wink as the pub thins out, you and a few others, never
many, just them he knew liked a drink and could hold a drink and
wouldn't make noisy cunts of their selves, shouting and pissing about
until coppers come banging at the door.

Draw the curtains,
kill the jukebox,
dim the lights,
bolt the door,
take a perch
at the bar, lads.

"I remember one Saturday come in here in such a fuckin' shithouse state after a lock-in the Duke and the gaffer goes to me –"

"Why you always banging on about that cunt? He's fuckin' dead."

"I know he's fuckin' dead."

"He hated me."

"He was good to me."

"Yeah, well he hated me, and his fuckin' wife an' all.
Then sold us this shithole, well over the fuckin' odds."

"Tidy little business when we bought in."

"Fuckin' ain't now is it, whose fault's that? Not fuckin' mine!"

Fucking nothing is your fault is it cunt?

"Oh, and that fat bastard's saying how he wants to take orders and cash up front now."

"What fat bastard?"

"With the van. Reckons he got stuck with a load of Glen's after some bloke got blinded off a bottle he got off him."

Glen's. It was Glen's, Boozeland, two the 20.

"He reckons how it wasn't the vodka it was something else, but he don't know what."

"How much was he after for the rest of it?"

"Already flogged on, I asked an' all, but he's pissed off 'cos he lost out."

"Suppose it's fair enough then."

"This'll be the last of that brandy though."

"Thank fuck."

"There was a fire, they was meant to go somewhere else..."

Took me years to work out that half the time landlords just want a pint in a pub like everyone else. A laugh and talk shit, have a pint and split a bag of nuts.

Always thought a lonely fucking job that, in some ways.
You'd never think so, especial if the pub was busy,
and the best of 'em are always larger than life,
but that was half a lot of front.

Can't be a mouse handling a room full of pissed up cunts night after night.

Imagine that! Watching everyone piss it up and you having to watch. I'd go fuckin' mad in half hour. They want a pint in a pub Saturday night just like
you and gob off bollocks about telly and sport and flying saucers a few hour.

And you didn't mind because it was better than going home and creeping upstairs trying not to wake mum and dad, or your wife and daughter, later.

Soft key in the lock,
and turn the latch slow,
soft step on the stair,
so no-one need know.

Bloke in the Duke reckoned he should have been this big star or something like, and every lock-in he'd be on about how him and his whole fucking family had been some sort of clubland turn, all singing and dancing, never got their fucking due, swizzed out of a go on Opportunity Knocks all that.

The Von Craps we called 'em, and they was a load of fucking rubbish from Burnley or somewhere like.
Him and the kids had these fucking great beaming white buck teeth.

And we was an audience for him and the whole clan.
Doing songs and impressions and jokes and fucking all kinds while we was nodding at the bar, clapping and making out to laugh,
because we wasn't up for going home just yet.

Proper lock-ins he'd have, all-nighters, and you'd roll home,
past Sunday's milk floats and paperboys at dawn.

Done a flit one night, the whole fucking Von Craps,
and turned out they'd not been paying for any of the pies or butties or fuck all of the bits of food they put on.

An odd pie.
Not from here, they were shit. His missus was alright to be fair. Manc.

"You was there with us, it was Christmas."

"I was where with you?"

"Last time I went in a pub, when that gang started in on us."

"That was fuckin' years ago with the Gaffer, you thumped a carol singer with a tambourine."

"Nah, the Gaffer was fuckin' dead."

"He dragged you out before you got twatted you dozy cunt."

"What, five or summat year back? That fucker was cold in the ground, pal."

"Oh hold on..."

"This was them in the uniforms wouldn't stop shouting when I told 'em to."

"The Sally Army, yeah."

"That's 'em, one minute she's fucking bawling and ringing a bell down my ear, next there's a couple of right big bastards on us."

"You fuckin' hit her."

And they was on you, dickhead, not on me, on you. Aye, I remember that now. Fucking downed my pint, and yours, and walked, and left 'em at it.

The Gaffer might've give enough toss for you to drag you out but I don't. They could have fucking killed you right there for all I care, and prayed for you at same time, them lot.

Fucking bad marge in my mouth.

"Think of all the money we've saved buying from shops since then."

"We didn't save it though did we? Fucking lot slashed up one wall or other."

"Yeah, but I was having a White Force other night – "

"Oh, was that the day when we got that White Force deal at BoozeMasters?"

"Could've been..."

Could've been my fuckin' arse. I knew he'd snuck a bottle off, walking out all hunched over with his arms wrapped round his self moaning about his guts.

"Yeah, I stopped off there on way back mine, 'cos it was such a good deal."

"Aye, we got through 'em quick though, 12 in two day."

"Goes down easy don't it? And I thought... I can't believe people throw their fucking money over the bars when for price of three pints you can have six litres of this, and it don't taste that bad."

"Sticks in my throat."

"Aye me an' all, but at eight per cent for that price…"

That white cider is rotten shit, I'd steer clear if I could, me. It bends your head. You see stuff, and all I taste is bacon. Greasy smoky bacon. They have to be fucking giving it away before I take a look, but they do a fair bit. That White Force six litres for six quid at BoozeMasters bit back, and we overdone it, to be honest, for a day or two, with a dozen. Minus whatever he slipped home. I just took one, me, soft cunt.

Frost, white,
carbon, ice,
White Ace,
Carbon White,
White Star,
Carbon Frost,
White Force
Frosty Jack,
Zeppelin.

"It was years ago, with me, sat in one night just when Zeppelin first come out, them big blue bottles, and I got halfway down one and thinks… you will never waste money in a fuckin' pub again. And I never."

"When was that?"

"Fuck knows. You remember that flat I had in Bird Street a few weeks?"

"When?"

"About 10 year back."

"You've been in pubs since then."

"Oh aye for a quick pint if I'm there, but never since that to get shitfaced."

"You was fuckin' shitfaced when you winded that Sally Army lass!"

"What's she fuckin' screamin' down me ear for then?"

They're one of them drinks where if you do a heavy stint on it then start back in on it next day you're back where you was the night before almost right off, like it stays in you waiting to wake up.
And if you stick on it a while you don't half see some stuff.

Not like the gin demons, as what they used to call 'em, we've all had them. You've only ever seen them when you've really hammered it and nodded off, I've found, then woke up sudden.

Spinning in the dark not remembering where or who you are or anything you see shadows different, like me and that soldier I kept seeing at the foot of the bed at night, in the trenchcoat, and I can't see but I know he's covered in mud.

White Force and them ain't that. Cider stuff feels like it's inside your head, not out, while you're wide awake, comes on out of nowhere, just out your thoughts.

"I don't mind it cold."

"Aye, cold is better."

"Fairly refreshing, if you get it down it fast."

That's why you have the ones in the doorways screaming now and then, like they do, if you've seen 'em, asleep or awake the same, struggling against things you can't see.

You look, next time, always be a three litre bottle all crumpled up like a blue plastic bag in their lap with a few inch sloshing about it.
Squashies they call 'em...

"I shotgunned three cans of White Lightning in the big park once and couldn't find my way out."

"When you was a kid?"

"This summer, I went down for a walk about late on because I was hot."

"Ain't done that in a bit."

"Me neither, but this kid had a knife so I give him a can for a borrow."

"Good swings that park had."

"I rolled down a banking through trees in the dark."

"Me and the missus went there first night we met, down the old bandstand..."

"I'm going shotgun a Kestrel are you?"

"Nah, you're alright."

"Fuck off it'll be a laugh."

Scared the shit out of me that fucking soldier because the first few times you don't know he ain't real and I thought he'd come for us.
Up out of bed like a jack-in-the-box trying twat him with the lamp, pissing while I done it, wet the bed, all over the carpet, screamed the fucking house down.

Woke her up, woke the kid up, wailing and lashing out for two or three minute, more, fucking awful.

Never caught me that bad again though, once or twice more, similar, but by the end I was just laying there watching him.

Began to think he was a ghost or something, but he wasn't, or if he was he only come out when I was shitfaced.

I woke her up and tried to show her, a few time, anyhow, but he wasn't there for her, just me, and when we both looked it was gone.

Never no different,
never done nothing,
never moved a muscle,
standing there,
looking down the bed.

Seen him a lot that Christmas she took the kid away.
I think he was looking,
but never saw his eyes,
his head hung low
and his helmet brim
cast a black shadow.

"Bppf-eayah."

"You what?"

Fuck shit this Dundee –

"Where's the bucket-bpf."

"Out back, I've been on it."

"Give us a bag."

"Eh?"

"Give us a BWAWK!"

"Ha ha, you dirty bastard!"

"Bwaa-AAAWK!"

"Ha ha ha haaah!"

Rancid marge, rancid marge and bitter burnt nuts and brandy,
taste that fucking brandy, from me arse to the top of me fucking head.

Fucking hell, never get used to puking do you? Always shakes you up.
Does me anyway, and I'm sick a lot with the way I am.
Eyes go, pissing out water and hot like they're full of nettles,
and snot fucking squirts out me nose.

Mind it's not so bad when there's plenty to come out like this.
Worst is when you empty yourself and keep going, like yesterday,
on and on, snot and tears drool off your face and belly wrecked
from pumping.

"Ha ha, that doddery old bastard's probably spewing his back in his
granny flat now! And the little bald bird."

"Nah, it's been the brandy done us, too fuckin' rich for me hernia."

"If she's give some her dog the mangy fucker's probably wretched its fuckin' wheels off!"

"It was that fuckin' brandy, I knew it was, the cake's – BWAWWK!"

"Ha ha, get it all out you and we'll have a shotgun."

Course, somewhere the Gaffer is telling me never to cut corners ain't he, but it was alright for him, his fridge never went fucked.

And if it did he was making enough brass to get it fixed.
Or get a new one. That one was new.
Last thing he bought in here before his stroke.

A little money machine this place, still, back then, even more when I started.
Thousand large whites a week rolled out of here alone. Two thousand!
Don't have a fucking clue, to be honest,
but I could have told you back then, to a dozen or so.

Lovely house, they had, the Gaffer and Alice, on the ridge, big garden out back and front, new Rover every year or two. It was only them two, wasn't it, and this shop did them alright. I think they had a nice life.

"You done?"

"I reckon."

"Ha ha, hole goes down the bottom of the can, don't it?"

"Yeah..."

"This'll fuckin' sort you out."

"I'm not bothering."

"Fuck off, I am, it'll be a laugh."

"You said it was all Kestrel now."

"It is."

"You've got Tennents."

"Last one this, it'd fell down the back."

"I ain't shotgunning this."

Always wondered who got all their dough.
Alice had no family I knew of, the Gaffer neither, they only had each
other, I'd have known.

Probably had someone somewhere though. People do. Or give it to
charity. Fucking donkeys or something. Good luck to 'em.
Them and the fucking donkeys wherever they are, wherever
donkeys go.

Course, that cunt reckoned we'd get a look in,
called the pair of 'em fit to burn when we never,
but how can you be arsed about shite like that?

The dead can do as they fucking like,
you've nowhere to go with your bullshit have you?

And why the fuck should they chuck some at us any road?
It ain't like we'd been anything much to 'em once this place changed
hands. We never helped or went much.
Two blokes they took on then sold on to.

One day people are every day,
next day once a year.
Bet fourth or fifth time

I seen the Gaffer since
dragged him out of here,
he was in a fucking box
and me in my dark suit.
They done enough for us when they was here. For me, for certain, for
fuck's sake. Teddy bear bigger than she was they got my little 'un one
birthday.

It was round the house for years, they never took it. She never took
to it.

We might still have it somewhere. In the little room that was mine,
once.

Went off the fucking rails
when first they fucked off,
nearly fucking offed myself,
really fucking tried,
with the ale, on and off.

And they helped me, for all the good it did.

Bet a fucking lot must've gone keeping Alice in that last place she was
in. Lovely place she went to, not some grey council shithole like I'll
be in.

Hers had all trees around, up behind the church, and she was there
for a good few year too, getting treated after her mind went, well, had
total gone, gone last time I seen her, and that was before she went
there, on her own in that house, after the funeral.

That went straight up for sale, and sold straight off, a lovely house
it was, and next time I went past that way there was a bloke playing
football with a little lad laughing his head off. Do kids laugh as much
now? Fucking hope so.

Should have gone up see her in there I know, but I knew what she'd say and what could I say to her?

She started forgetting everything long before the Gaffer went.
Fuck me, at his funeral she was asking over and over where the missus was, and where's the little girl, because oh, the Gaffer had loved her so much and he'd be so sad to know she wasn't here!

And looked at me,
red eyes pleading,
for this one thing,
we'd both lost.
I ain't fucking seen her in 15-odd year, Alice, remember?
You said I was a fucking idiot and should put the bottle down and sort my ideas out if I wanted her back and I did for a bit but didn't last, did I?
And you seen all that, all that go down the fucking drain for yourself, bit by bit, so you know well enough, love.
Or you knew.
Fucking hope I go senile me. Wipe it all away and look out the window.

Fucking lovely woman. She helped me and the missus, they both did.
For all the good it did.

"Told you them scones'd go alright."

"They'll all fuckin' regret it."

"Says you with your fuckin'
Dundee cake dripping down
your shirt."

"It was the brandy."

"Right, I'm doing this."

"We should get some bitters in..."

"Graalggle!"

Fucking state of that, half of it coming out his nose.

"Don't try and breathe you daft cunt."

"Graahk!"

You don't half feel it though. Used do 'em all the time when we was kids, soon as we got showed how. Fuck it, I'll have one while we are.

"Where's the knife?"

"Gwaaah!"

"Where's the –"

"Fuck me..."

Why in fuck has he brought this whopping great bastard through for pricking shotgun holes in a can?
Used to use this chopping fucking onions by the 5lb bag!

Bawling your fucking eyes out for the mince and onion
and the cheese and onion and the meat and potato.
Gaffer never, though, but he had jam-jar glasses.

"Me head's full of lager."

"Fuck!"

"You're bleeding."

"Give us some fuckin' bags!"

That's down to the bone that, right the bone, felt the scrape along, right up me arm, and sharp enough, but jagged, felt the drag.

"Fuck ow fuck."

"You're fuckin' bleedin' everywhere you soft cunt."

"Give us some fuckin' bags."

"Here – shove it in that."

"A fuckin' loaf? Fuck off."

"'It'll soak it up won't it?"

"Bollocks!"

That don't feel bad as it goes. Soft and cool.
Moist. Put it under some water in a minute.

"If I pour brandy down the loaf it'll be like anaesthetic."

"Fuck off with that brandy and open my can."

"I mean antiseptic."

"I'll run the tap on it, just pop me can, I've only one hand."

"You not shotgunning it?"

"With half me fingers fuckin' off? No."

Thank fuck it's the left.
Copped worst burn before an' all, so I've been lucky there.

Never use it for nothing. I ain't going to be icing no wedding cakes in

the next few hour and needing to squeeze a bag.
Never did much of that any road.
Gaffer said I didn't have the touch, and he was right enough.

I could do your basic ice, but all the bits that make 'em special,
all the fine things that make 'em beautiful, the gaffer'd finish up.

Odd it was seeing a chunky bastard like him weaving and waving his
pipe over the ice and these pretty little swirls and flowers and that
flowing out, never stopping, only to change a nozzle over.
That cunt wasn't so bad neither, pains to say, and the gaffer'd sooner
leave him to finish up a birthday cake or whatever before me.

Never the wedding cakes though.
Or the anniversaries or the special birthdays, the ones that mean
something. Gaffer always finished the important cakes his self.

Cakes people remember,
point cameras at,
clap to see cut,
cakes that are shared
among hundreds,
family and friend,
pieces set aside to send
to those who can't be there,
and fragments saved a lifetime.

If you think about it, every milestone in lift comes with a special cake,
except one.

The one you reach but don't pass.

Mum had a piece of her wedding cake in among her bits when I was
helping tidy away her bits with Dad, once she'd gone, a single finger,
wrapped in white tissue and a cotton hankie, in a white box with the
little couple, which was a fucking miracle really because Dad inhaled

cake like a fucking Hoover.

If there was half a cake in the house when he rolled home he'd sniff it out and there was fucking crumbs by the time he'd got his boots off, and he'd bash and shake the tin to drink them down an' all most times.

That little bit of cake surviving all them years was a fucking miracle.

Probably went out with all her other stuff in the end, I didn't keep much.
Her ring, for a while. A picture of me and Adrian, black and white, in the yard. We could have been twins, then, but last time I seen him he still had his hair.
Me and dad lost ours.

Brung the bit of cake in to show the Gaffer and he reckoned he'd made it. Probably did, she was here when they wed, only left when I come along.
They'd have just paid for the materials, the fruit, like us.

"Let's have a look then."

"Still fuckin' bleeding."

"Looks sore that. Mash bread into it."

"Fuckin' stinks this."

"The yeast was gone. Blue dust on it."

Need stitches them but I ain't going nowhere in this state, sick down my front stinking of ale. It's horrible. Even when you hold yourself together people treat you different anyway, soon as they get a smell of you.

And I do hold myself together, that's the thing, I do. Not like that cunt, me, blabbing and shouting his mouth off, on his arse half the time.

I hold my drink. You'd never know I was drunk if you seen me but couldn't smell me because I hold it. I hold myself, always have, always been able.

Most people was once, and they drank enough.
Always been knobheads like that cunt, making an exhibition, but when I started going out I'd have a suit on most times, most did, and so you never hardly seen cunts rolling round outside the chippy biting lumps off each other to impress some slag with a shoe off and her knickers showing.

Thing of holding your drink
ain't how much you can drink,
but how much you can drink
while not being a cunt.

Besides, if you ain't a gobshite drink won't make you a gobshite. If you are everyone'll want to smash your head round before having ten pint.

Drink don't change people who have nothing to hide just shows you what's there to begin with, only up close. And if you have got something to hide you won't for long, because nothing makes an honest man of a bullshitter like a fucking skinful.

That cunt has nothing to hide but you still want to smash his head round. He's a gobshite, one of them don't take ten pint to find out.

"I can't feel me fingertips."

"You've probably cut some nerves. I done that on that finger there years back trying get two frozen burgers apart with a carving knife when I was pissed and it's totally dead from there up."

You must have stuck it in your fucking neck an' all because so is your head.

"Oww!"

"What the fuck you doing?"

"I used be able to bite that as hard as I wanted. Or that one."

"Give it a bite."

"Nothing. See?"

"See what?"

"This – See? Nothing."

"You've drew blood."

"Can't feel a fucking thing."

First time had a pint with him in a pub, very first time, first Saturday he was on here, down the club just after the results, nearly had a scrap with one of my mates over fuckin' nothing.

Shouting and sloshing his pint about and a big blob of beer went on – what the fuck was his name now?
Fuck we come right through big school an' all.

Any road, on his bird's white skirt.
They was playing snooker and this cunt starts shouting the odds about something being up with his cue and waves half a pint down Jimmy's – that's him, Jimmy O'Neil – lass who's sat down the side.

Didn't apologise or nothing and Jimmy pulls him up on it, but only half joking because we're all half a day into a drink Saturday teatime and everyone's fairly rolling, and next thing this cunt's going 'car park, now, fuckin' now', with a big pair of stupid platform boots on.

Even ten pints on down the road Jimmy'd have broke his fucking back for him, he'd been on the steel since he was 14 and was a brick shithouse at 17, but instead he talked him round and the cunt ended up apologising and being alright rest of the night, but I marked his fucking card there and then.

Still see Jimmy about time to time but he don't seem to twig me.

Mind I've changed a lot more than he has, he could be 30,
and we both wed youngish and stopped knocking about fairly short order.
I ended up doing most of my drinking on me own,
then, and then with that cunt.

He's done alright for his self, Jimmy, there are vans with his name on.
Be 35 year since we had a pint.
20 since we said hello.
Maybe a wave
10 year ago.

"Fuck me is getting early dark, not much gone two."

"The fucking clock stopped."

"When?"

"Fuck knows. Then."

"So it ain't getting dark that early?"

"I don't know what time is."

"What's the clock in the back say?"

"Have a look, I ain't dragging this bloody bread everywhere."

"You having another brandy?"

"Just a splash, I'm feeling it. Bit more..."

We might as well turn that sign over, no fucker is coming in now.
Gone three, at least? No fucker.
Let's get the fuck home.

Used to get the odd schoolkids wandering in seeing if any cakes was going off and cheap, and Alice'd usually find 'em something, but they don't seem so arsed any more.

Half 'em get drove to and fro,
so don't get to wander about any road,
so much any more.

These days you have to watch for perverts. Parents want to get 'em home where it's safe.
No danger like that when mine was little, she played out in the street all hours. Probably safer outside than she was at home.

That's where all the accidents happen, ain't it?

"Just four."

"Is that clock right?"

"It's fuckin' tickin'."

That ain't why we burn stuff then. Maybe you just stop looking at clocks.
And then time flies.
The buns are in,
cracking on,
put your head down
cut some scone,
roll it out
crack a can,
cut 'em out,
have a drink,
wash 'em up,
bang 'em in,
crack a can,
an hour's gone –
and there's smoke.

First off the days are all the same, but by the end it's the minutes.

"Best day this has been in a bit."

"Eh?"

"There'll be twenty quid or about gone through that till."

"Aye, do that every day and we might last another week."

"Glad them scones went alright."

"Egg-wash, Gaffer swore by it."

"They won't taste that bad."

"Fuckin' eat one then."

"That shotgun's blew me out..."

"I'm turning the sign over."

"Give it another half hour..."

"What you expecting a fuckin' coach party?"

"Kids drop in don't they after school for stale bits..."

"They've all gone home, the fuckers knock off about half two now."

I'm sure we was at school 'til later but I can't think when it was.
Half four or summat?

There always seemed half-decent crowd in the beer yard of the pub
other side of the wall on the path to the top gate on the way home.

Mind you they was three o'clock closing then, because we mostly
used be in for a few knocking off back when there were the lasses to
clean up and lock up.

Us and the binmen, posties and early shifters.
And there was afternoon lock-ins, we had plenty.
Same rules though, inside, at the bar.

Maybe I'm thinking of playtimes.

"What was that pub up the side of Severn Street Juniors?"

"I was fuckin' barred from there for nothing."

Oh I bet it was nothing you fuckin' shitheap.

"Was it the Red Ox?"

"Nah that was same side about 200 yard on.
Fuckin' barred from there an' all, but that were fair enough."

"The Grapes."

"You can't shit in a snug, even if you catch it in a pot, I was in the wrong."

"Were it the Grapes?"

"That's it, that Scouse twat behind bar for thirty fuckin' year."

"More, my dad reckoned he'd been in there when me grandad was a regular."

"Fuckin' hated me that old cunt."

"He must have been 70 when I started going in."

"Nobody seen me kick that fuckin' sink off in the bogs, but I got blamed."

"I remember that. All the water gashed out and fucked the carpet in the pool room."

"That's it, ain't long left school me, we wasn't mates then."

We ain't fucking mates now you fucking arsehole cunt.

"No proof or nothing, and I hadn't been boasting it or nothing, but who gets fuckin' barred?

"You."

"Fuckin' me."

"I'm turning that sign, I'm knackered, want to get home, look at me fuckin' hand."

"Nobody seen, there wasn't a soul in there, when I went in I checked."

"It must be half-four, nobody's coming in now."

"Scouse cunt, him and his fuckin' wife."

"I'm ready for going home."

"Just give it another quarter hour some of them kids from that home down there wander about these streets until all hours."

"There ain't been one wander in here for fucking years."

"It's trying to rain, people come in for shelter."

Never wants to go home these days. Like a ghost ten year ago, vanishing off leaving me to side away. Now he's always hanging on and trying stop open long as he can, dawdling about when we're tinning up and that.

Just four walls and his self waiting. I don't think he has a fucking telly. And it's probably a fucking shithole an' all.

Never seen his digs. Not these any road. Plenty of others.
Must have rolled through 30 pokey slums in the time I've known him, and helped him move in or out of half of 'em, all of 'em, until I told him to fuck off and find another mug.
Shitholes, last dozen or so, such as I seen.
Had house with a lass for a bit, but something happened, fuck knows what. Reckoned she was a bigger pisshead than he was but I'd be surprised,
and after that he ain't stopped more than six month anywhere.

Bet I ain't seen last ten places he's lived.

Always inviting us round and have a drink, but fuck that, no chance.
See enough of the cunt without sitting in his shitty bedsit passing a bottle to and fro on the edge of his fucking pit because there's no chairs.
Done enough of that.

"Fifteen fuckin' minute, but I'm going start tinning up."

"Fuckers won't see what we've got on offer then."

"What fuckers?"

"You can't do it any road with one hand in a fuckin' loaf bleeding to fuck, you'll get your blood all over the cakes."

"You'll have to do it then."

"I will, once we've shut. Brandy?"

Fucking hell.

"Just a splash."

"There?"

"Top us up, have we got plasters?"

"We did have, there was a first aid box."

"Where's that?"

"Fuckin'... Christ knows."

"I'm going run it under the tap."

They're some deep cuts. Fucking ring finger half through.
Might have to get them seen to. Unless there's plasters.

Or a rag. There's a rag.

Don't get many cuts, not now. Don't have the same big knives
chopping about. You don't once you stop doing savouries, and even
before, ten year since we was doing more than a dozen-odd pie a day,
at most, very most.

Back when we shifted pies quick as we made 'em there was big knives
everywhere with all that meat to slice and onions and carrots and
spuds to chop up, pound after fucking pound of 'em.

Burned is what we get now, as a rule. A lot. Where'd you even start
looking?

"Where'd you see it last?"

"Eh?"

"The plasters box, where was it?"

"In there, in the back."

"When?"

"Fuckin'... years ago. I drank the TCP."

"Where?"

"Don't ask me I ain't cut myself..."

There's no booze in TCP neither so fuck knows what he got out of that.
Fresh breath and bad guts for a week.
Mind there's been some shit drunk all round in here, as and when
we've run short, and the offie's been shut, or it's been pissing down,
so I can't talk.

Never my idea like, left alone I can go without a fair while, but he
starts pulling his hair out after five minute and then anything goes and
if he's having some I'm having some, because I'll have paid half for it.
He'll be a doorway meth, him, one day, once this place gives out,
bet your bottom bollock. Headed for a doorway his whole fuckin' life,
him, and I just hope I live long enough to watch.
Even if it's from the next fucking doorway along.

"What's that?"

"A tea-towel."

"Didn't know we had any tea towels."

"We've got one."

"We'll look after that..."

"Where'd you put the tins?"

"Where's this, where's that – why should I have to know all that shit?"

"You set up out here this morning you cunt, you must have had the tins."

"Oh aye. What's she after?"

Christ she ain't much meat on her. Not a lot of her. Young old face on it. Press her nose any harder against that glass it'll be through the window. It's raining.

"What's she fuckin' gawping at?"

"She could stand to eat a cake or two her."

"I've seen her, she hangs round the precinct with her fuckin' hand out."

"She's coming in."

"Keep an eye out for her on the fuckin' rob."

Rob what you cunt? It's all behind here, what shit there is.
Fuck me she's like a bunch of wet broom-handles.
Can't be 16 or much more.

"Can we help you love?"

"Have you got any jobs?"

"Not for you y'fuckin' junkie, sling yer hook."

"I'm not a junkie I'm trying find a job."

"We're alright for smackheads, on yer fuckin' way."

"I never... I need 43p for me bus."

No age at all.

"How old are you love?"

"Fuck off y'pervert."

"On yer fuckin' way or I'll drag yer out!"

Never seen kids like that round here, once. Not so long ago.
Not kids.
There was always tramps and that, proper tramps an' all,
big beards and a fucking stick and hankie on their shoulder.

One chopped kindling for butties and brews. Gingerbeard. He'd
been in the war, dad said he remembered him. Bit of a local hero
he reckoned, when he'd been a lad, won a medal near the end for

something he'd done in Belgium.

"She might tell the coppers on you now you dickhead."

"Tell 'em what?"

"After her age! Why you after her fuckin' age?"

"Seemed young to be in that state is all."

"You'll be in a fuckin' state when she tells pigs you tried to fuck her or whatever you was up to."

"I'm turning that sign over, we're shut."

"You'll be shut, in a fuckin' nonce box, mate, slashed up to fuck."

There was them tramps, two or three of them, and a couple of town alkies, everyone knew, but they was all fucking old an' all.
Not kids.

Seen that Bunny Mercer asleep face down in the bus shelter right outside the big Co-Op one afternoon with his slacks full of fresh shit when I was a kid and all the old ladies with their shopping trolleys tutting and waiting for their bus in the rain miles away from the shelter. But he must have been 50-odd. He had a fucking suit on half the time. Tatty, twisted up and full of shit like, but a suit. Something happened to his wife I think. Dad remembered him...

But never kids,
not like her,
not all over,
not every day,
already set out
on wasting away.

"That precinct's gone to shit with all them scumbags hanging round it begging and that."

"There's been fuck all there for a bit to be fair."

"The fuckin' bogs are revolting. I knelt down in there and when I stood up there's a fuckin' needle hangin' out of me shin."

"What you kneeling down in there for?"

"I didn't feel s'well."

"There's still some good deals at that offie in there."

"BoozeZone."

"Nah, that ain't BoozeZone."

"SupaBooze?"

"SupaBooze, aye."

"They all hang round outside there and try grab booze off the pissheads."

"Poor little fuckers though."

"One tried grabbing a Zeppelin off me once, but I fuckin' hit him and legged it."

"It's Boozeland."

"That's it."

You left school, got a job, everyone got a job, somewhere, went out drinking, lads met lasses, got yourselves on the council waiting list, got wed, settled down, and that was your little set-up.

Most did, any road. Always a few born scrotes, course there was, but by and large that's how it went. Then you started fucking your life up from there.

Takes longer when you're older because you're busier.
And sometimes people don't fuck everything up but the fates hit 'em and fuck everything up any road.

So piss-pots was generally older. Everyone had a chance.

Bunny must have been old as me now.
The tramps was all older blokes an' all.
But these bits of kids you see...

Like they dropped out fully fucked from the off.

The factories have gone, along with every kid round here with anything about 'em from the minute they put two and two together. By the time half the rest crack that it's too late and they're stuck.

Same as our Adrian done is that. No age when he darted off, not even 21. Took one job, led to another, next he's emigrated and made a good life for his self, where it was he went, to Canada.

Met a lovely lass.
He only come back the once, as I know of, for Mum's funeral.
I didn't meet her, it was winter and she'd been scared to fly.

His funeral was over there, but I couldn't get. Dad went.
Showed me the pictures of Adrian's family when he came down to visit, and said we should both go, but I never seen him again.

I have a nephew and a niece, over there. Grown-up.
I saw a photograph.

They were tiny in the snow, back then.

"You want a splash of this?"

"I'm turning that fucking sign over, let's get sided away."

"You fancy going for a pint?"

"I'm going home. Where's them tins?"

"All that talking about pubs, I fancy a pint."

"Ain't fucking stopping you."

Ain't coming with you neither you cunt.
And if there's a pub in this town you ain't still barred from I'll eat hay
with a fucking donkey.

He's the new Bunny Mercer, him, he's shit his self in a shop, I seen him.

Maybe I'm a Bunny an' all. Not shit in a shop, never, this one aside, but
you never know what people are thinking of you, not from a distance.

The fucking relief to turn that latch. Turn that sign from open to closed.

Out of here in 15 minutes, up that hill and home half hour.

Should close earlier.
Long days without lasses to tidy up and shut up.
Full 12 hours that. For a tenner, today, if we're lucky.

Only one's ever in here afternoons any road are fuckers bringing back
stuff they bought so that's them shut out 'til tomorrow anyway, and
we can crack on they're stale so it's hard to say then.
Nothing stays fresh forever love, am very sorry, all that,
offer 'em two of anything, call it quits.

"Pint of bitter'd settle your guts after that horrible cake."

"Nothing wrong with the cake, was the fucking brandy,
and me guts are alright now."

"They might have a fire lit in the Old England."

"Old England's long gone, every stone of it.
What's worth keeping from yesterday?"

"All of it, fuck it, I'd eat any of it."

"Them Viennese Fingers are going out, they look like some fucker's
booted 'em."

"I dropped the tin then kneeled on it when I tried pick it up,
they'll taste as good."

They wasn't bad actually. I had one.
Sold about six an' all, and not one come back.
We can still fucking do it. Just nobody seems to want it.

Hold up that were fucking yonks ago.

"How old are these?"

"They was around yesterday."

"We done these last week."

"Always good keepers."

"You want one?"

"I don't like eating once I've had a few drinks, you don't feel the drinks as much."

I'd be lying if I said I didn't think the same, half the time.
If you're going to eat get in early, have it at the bottom of your guts.
That was my mistake with the Dundee, I was already suffering.

Or you fall asleep and all the booze gets used up while you're asleep.

"I'm going for a pint, anyway, if you can be arsed."

"I can't."

"That Wetherspoons is cheap I've heard."

"You was never drinking in a pub again half hour ago."

"A pint's not drinking, is it? Is just a pint."

"I'm going home."

Feeling lonely are we?
Well fuck off pal, I'm lonely too, but I ain't that fucking lonely yet.
I'll have a look for that teddy bear tonight if there's nothing on.

Sure seen it upstairs,
can't remember when,
in the room that was hers,
away back then,
and little mine,
away back before,
there's all sorts in there,
behind that closed door.
Long time ago that was though.
Stopped looking in there long time ago. No point.
Can't see where else it could be. If not I'll just watch something.

If I can find anything.

"I'll buy you a pint, we've made twenty-four quid."

"Six quid of that's float."

"Twenty quid then. I'll buy you a pint."

"Stick it in the pot this brandy ain't going last forever. I hope."

"I'm having a pint anyway."

"Are you going to wash-up?"

"This bread ain't boxing itself."

"Neither are you, you're stood there necking brandy with your hand
in the till."

"Stop rushin' us! I'd tip it back in the bottle if I could..."

Sod all to wash-up any road, it'll keep 'til tomorrow.
Can't think we'll be making much anyway. This lot's not bad.
The Dundee and the scones and the flapjacks will pass for fresh again.

And the macaroons. And the ginger.

Maybe make a small few nice cakes. Some butterfly cakes.

"We'll do it tomorrow, there's fuck all."

"Yeah, save us some time..."

Christ, non-stop washing-up first day I walked in here. Never had your hands out of hot water for five hour, fingers like fucking prunes by time you was done, little shrivelled old man's faces.

Two of us washing up on Saturdays, then, they was that busy.
If you wasn't scrubbing tins and bowls and racks and knives and pins you was stacking 'em to dry.

And the Gaffer walking past every ten minute yanking the plug shouting 'We wash 'em in hot water here lad, not cold flour' and spinning the hot tap, scalding your bright red hands off again.

And then wiping down and sweeping up for hour! Left that shop like a new pin for Monday. And then out for the Saturday afternoon up town with a quid burning hole in your pocket. Not a care. Not fucking one.

"I'm going to... might as well finish this bottle off now."

"It's all yours."

"There's only a fuckin' bit!"

"Sup up, we're finished here."

"Fuckin' Christ! I'm trying to have a bloody drink and relax after work..."

"Thought you was going for a pint."

"Mmm, yeah, are you coming?"

"Nah, going home. Hand fuckin' killing me."

"I've just to nip in the back."

Aye, run and get your little stash, cunt. Had mine in me bag all day.

"What's that stuck up yer shirt?"

"Ohh, I have bad guts. What day are we?"

"Wednesday."

"Thought it was Thursday."

"Why?"

"I don't know. It felt it"

"Where you off for your pint then?"

"Thought I'd have a walk over the Old England."

"That's been –"

 No, you have a little walk. Get run over.

"Aye, was always nice in there. They might have a fire in."

"Aye it's cold enough. Fancy a pint then?"

"Nah, I'm going home."

"Getting darker earlier ain't it?

"See you tomorrow."

Always that to look forward to.

"Friday?"

"It's Thursday y'fuckin –"

Call it Friday, makes no odds. We're open Thursday and Friday. So long as you don't forget when Saturday is, for Sunday, and the new week to come.

Fucking get me up this hill...